THE HAWTHORNE UNIVERSITY WITCH HOLIDAY COLLECTION

BELTANE FIRE, SAMHAIN WITCH, & CANDY CRONE

A. L. HAWKE

PHANTOM HEART, LLC

ISBN: 978-1-953919-85-4

ISBN: 978-1-953919-79-3 (paperback)

This is a work of fiction. It comes directly from the author's imagination. Witchcraft is included to infuse a sense of realism to the novel, but in no way is it supposed to represent actual practicing witchcraft, witches or the religion of Wicca. The book also includes fictitious names, characters, places, and incidents. Any public names are used solely for creative purposes. Any resemblance to actual people, living or dead, or to companies, institutions, or locales is entirely coincidental or accidental.

Line edited by Stephanie Marshall Ward

Proofread by Alexa B., alexabooks.wixsite.com/authors

Cover Design © 2025 by Brosedesignz

Published by Phantom Heart, LLC

27702 Crown Valley Pkwy, STE D4 #201

Ladera Ranch, CA 92694

Printed and bound in the United States of America

First printing 2025

Learn more about A.L. Hawke at www.alhawke.com

Correspondence: contact@alhawke.com

❀ Created with Vellum

The Hawthorne University Witch Holiday Collection is available in this three book collection. Each standalone short story encompasses real occult and pagan practices and beliefs during the Easter, Halloween, and Christmas holiday seasons, amid Cadence's romantic, paranormal and ghostly adventures in a witchy university setting.

Happy Holidays & Enjoy!

A.L. Hawke

BELTANE FIRE

1

———

FIND SOMEONE WHO LOVES ME

I'm sitting on a wicker chair big enough for three on the backyard patio of the Billington frat house, flipping through my World Civ notes. It's warm and pleasant with a lovely full moon lighting the wild grass of the backyard and the surrounding trees of Hawthorne Forest. So most of the students are enjoying the outdoors. Normally I wouldn't mind—the front yard of the house is a creepy place to hang out at when you aren't surrounded by people, and the house is supposedly haunted. But I'm having a helluva time concentrating for my test tomorrow. I told Maddie I couldn't make it, but she insisted I come. Apparently, the May festival is super special in Hawthorne. Because Hawthorne is super weird.

I'm on Ramses II. Did you know that Ramses II is a pharaoh who reigned from 1303 to 1213 B.C.? Yep. This pharaoh, perhaps the most popular, lived to be ninety years old! That's really amazing for an ancient old guy. It's thought he might be the pharaoh who lived during the exodus of Moses in the Bible.

Shouts and laughter disrupt me again, along with the smell of burning embers. Usually I like the smell of burning wood, but this smoke is getting thick. The entire grassy field surrounding the two bonfires is glowing red. Tons of students are hanging around there, pushing each other, yelling stupidly, and laughing. Some are wearing creepy black masks with beaks, others have ornate flower arrangements on their heads, and a few are wearing antlers. Maddie told me that, for pagans, this time of year is like an upside-down Halloween.

Anyway ... Ramses II. Maybe Ramses II is so well known because he was an egomaniac? He put his face in stone everywhere, including the famous Abu Simbel temple. (I'll have to mention that in my essay.) I'm looking at a black-and-white photo of the Abu Simbel temple. Ramses's wife, Nefartari, was pretty big in Egyptian lore too. She was supposedly the most beautiful lady ever to marry a pharaoh. *Nefer* means beauty in ancient Egyptian.

A partier jumps onto the other side of my bench, shaking my notebook. It's not the first time. The last time it was a couple making out.

"Whatcha doing, bitch?" she asks, slapping my thigh. It's my roommate and best friend, Maddie. She's chewing gum with this really big grimace.

Our outfits are fun. She's wearing a garland of daisies over her long dark hair. She told me that one of her friends who's organizing the party, named Tammy, made the flower garland for her. Apparently, she made my garland too. And we're wearing matching white dresses that make us look like the Greek goddess Diana. It's cute and summery.

She places a red plastic cup in my hand.

"What's this?" I ask.

"Try it," she says with a wink.

My friend knows full well I'm not twenty-one, but I take a sip. Then I wrinkle my nose. It's dry and sharp, but very sweet. Too sweet.

"Yuck. What is it?"

"You're so cute, Katie." Maddie grabs me and holds me tight, laughing. "I love you."

"Yeah? But what is it?"

"Mead. A bit sharper than the youz. My friend made it."

"Mead is like fermented honey, right?"

She shrugs.

I sip it again. "It's not so bad. I guess I was expecting beer."

"So?" she asks with a shrug. "Whatcha reading?"

"The pharaohs of ancient Egypt. Did you know they drank mead in Egypt?"

She shrugs again as if to say she really couldn't give a shit.

"I told you I have an exam tomorrow. And finals after that."

"Kates, you're the only nerd I know who can still look good with her nose stuck in a notebook in the middle of a raging party. I need to get you some fake glasses. Why not lift those lovely eyes of yours and look around? Didn't I get you to come to this place to see guys? You're not gonna see anything burying your head in the ancient pharaohs."

Right then and there, two girls run past us giggling stupidly. One has a weird black druid cloak and dark makeup. The other is wearing practically nothing: a bikini bottom—*only* a bikini bottom. She's braless, boobs and all, but you can't be certain because her entire body, including her face, is painted red. But I clearly see breasts bobbing. They're heading for the two bonfires, of course.

"Well, there's a naked girl," I say, shaking my head and pointing. "Where's the guys?"

"Her body's painted, Katie," Maddie says, rolling her eyes.

Then Maddie takes a deep breath, leans back in the wicker chair, folds her arms, and stares out at all the people hanging around the bonfires. Before I can get back to the pharaoh, she heaves another long, deep sigh, playing up this pretense of being totally bored.

"What are you doing?"

"Hanging with my friend. If you want to be dull, then I'll just be boring with you. Go ahead. Read on."

"Okay, fine," I say, getting up. "What do you want to do?"

She looks at me with a sly smile and puts a finger to her chin, as if she doesn't know. "Well...we might be too late." She snatches my arm and drags me off the chair. "Come on. Let's go find out."

She shoves my notepad to a confused guy as he walks out of the house. She tells him to take very good care of my book or else. I don't know who the boy is, but Maddie apparently does. She knows everybody.

Then we walk across the backyard, dodging a few more bodies. I'm holding the mead I don't like in one hand and Maddie's pulling me with the other.

"Where are we going?"

"Got something to show ya."

It's a hilly yard, covered with wild grass, that eventually just blends into the woods. There are no boundaries, and we're soon traipsing through Hawthorne Forest. Hawthorne Forest surrounds our college for miles. But as I look back through some trees, I can still see the large three-story brick structure. The Billington House is the oldest house in Hawthorne. But now it's a fraternity house, and tonight the lights are on in every room and rock music is blaring with kids screaming. The party's raging inside, and the place is so packed that the yellow light flickers as bodies pass the windows.

As we move farther away, the music fades. People blend into the shadows under the full moon. And I just hear lots of talking. The smell of fire is replaced by the smell of pot. My eyes fall on a girl, lying under a tree. Her mouth is hanging open and her eyes are closed. It's so busy that people just walk past her. She's wearing a plaid skirt and a red sweater with Greek letters in gold. Maddie and I don't care for sororities.

"She okay?" I ask. I might not like 'em, but I don't want to see them hurt.

"She's dead," Maddie whispers in my ear. Then she blows a bubble of gum at me.

I freeze over the girl for a moment. Thankfully, she shifts position showing that she's alive.

"Come on, babe!" my friend says, tugging me. "We're gonna miss it."

"What? We're heading away from the party into the middle of the woods. I thought you wanted me to see the festival?"

"They're still preparing. There's more festivities this way. Trust me. Come on."

We pass another few tree trunks; these are darker. And here in the shadows I catch a couple groping and making out.

"I really need my notes, Maddie. I outlined all my stuff for the test tomorrow. If not tonight, I want to go over it again tomorrow morning."

"Don't worry," she says, chewing gum that smells like spearmint, "Trent is like you. He's always got his nose stuck in books. And he's got a crush on me. He does anything I ask him. Your notebook couldn't be in better hands. Trust me."

We climb over a grassy hill and it's brighter. At the bottom of the hill a small valley opens into Hawthorne Forest. I can see shadows of trees for miles. At the base of the hill there are four large torches on wooden poles. Even though it's still the backyard of the Billington House, it seems secluded. A small group of about twenty students, holding beer bottles or plastic cups, are talking around a branchless tree.

"Finish up, everyone," cries someone with a laugh. She's a dark-skinned girl wearing a white dress and garland like Maddie and me. "When you're done writing your greatest wish in the world at the end of your ribbon, follow the lead or you'll tangle and fuck everything up. Follow the person in front of you. The frat boys want us to do a real good job for their hall. Right, Bryce?"

"Hi Tamms," Maddie says, touching the girl on her back. "This is my bestie, Cadence, I was telling you about. Cadence, this is my friend Tammy. Tammy organized this."

"Hi," I say with a wave. "Fun party."

I sip more of the mead. It's not that bad, actually. It has a sweet wine-like taste. I'm actually starting to like it.

"Hi Cadence," Tammy says more quietly, handing me the end of a red ribbon. "Welcome and happy Beltane." She hugs me really tight. She has a kind smile. "Have you two decorated a maypole before?"

I shake my head.

"I've done these ever since I was a kid. It's a lot of fun. We start at the top of the tree with the wreath and streamers. Write your greatest wish at the bottom of your streamer. Just a sentence. Keep it private and only to yourself. Then, when ready, dance in step with us. We picked a spot where no one should bother us, deep in the woods. The pole will remain here for months with your note. My hope is that your wish will be granted for you, Cadence."

She seems real nice. Maddie smiles at me because my BFF can read my mind. She told me about Tammy, and I think she knows I already like her.

I put my cup on the ground and take a pen from my jeans pocket. Yes, I have a pen. I'm a college student. And yes, like Maddie said, I'm a nerd. Actually, I have two pens. I hand Madison one.

I bite my lip, looking around, thinking of what to say. Then I make sure no one's looking and quickly scribble, deliberately making the words barely legible: *Find someone who loves me.*

The moment I finish writing the last word, I'm startled by someone tapping the back of my shoulder. I turn and gasp. Under the flickering torchlight is this tall blue-eyed boy with slicked-back, perfectly combed dark hair. He's wearing another of those really weird black druid cloaks, but under it is a preppy button-down and slacks. He's smiling. And he's hot as hell.

My face feels hot. I don't think he can notice in the flickering torchlight, but I kinda step back. Then I feel even more embarrassed, worrying about him seeing me blush. My skin is naturally tanned, you know, but my cheeks can still light up like a cherry. I'm hoping, no, *praying*, that this guy didn't read the stupid thing I just scribbled.

"Be careful what you wish for," he breathes. "Your wish will come true. All wishes come true by Samhain after our ceremony with Cernunnos."

...Okay.

"Hope so," I blurt. *God! Please tell me he didn't read what I wrote!* "I just jotted down the first thing that came into my mind," I mumble with a shrug.

"The words manifest from our magic as we circle the pole," he says with a nod. Then he sticks out his hand for a shake. "I'm Bryce." He looks over at Maddie, still shaking my hand. "And you guys are late. When you both are ready, we're going to dance."

Dance with Bryce. How nice...

"Cadence," I belatedly say to him. Maddie giggles stupidly behind him, and I want to kill her. Then Bryce seems to hold my hand a little longer than usual.

"Got mine written," Maddie says. "Hey, Cadence, how 'bout you? What'd you write?"

"I thought it was private?" I ask, pulling away from tall-dark-and-handsome.

"Why? Did you write something you don't want us to know?"

Bitch.

She's got a stupid grin and, of course, the whole group is staring at me.

"How've you been, Madison?" Bryce asks with a chuckle. I tell you, Maddie knows everyone in Hawthorne. "Did you like my mead?"

"You made that?" I ask.

"Um-hmm." He nods. "Home brewing is my hobby. Got the taste for it from some of my chemistry friends."

"You guys done chitchatting?" asks Tammy. "Come on, we've got to hurry up or I'll miss my part in the fire ceremony."

But Bryce is gazing into my eyes. He has these really gorgeous blue eyes and, for a moment, as I look deeply into them, I just die. I know it's stupid, but I do. He smiles really sweetly. At me.

Cadence. Huh. Yeah what? Cadence.

Okay, he doesn't say all that, but I imagine he does. Then I think of how stupid I'm being. He's just a boy—a tall older guy with a square jaw, broad shoulders, and these gorgeous bright blue eyes.

"Grab the edge of your streamer, okay?" Tammy says to the group. "And chug down or drop your drinks. Let's go."

Bryce nods to a few people behind him, in the trees, that I didn't notice before. They start playing drums. Then he surprises me by looking deeply into my eyes again. Because he has to. Everyone is facing the person next to them. Maddie's behind me.

"Ready, Cadence?" he asks, facing me.

Uh, with you? For sure.

The drumbeat is hypnotic. We walk slowly around the tree. But the drum's rhythm speeds up as we get accustomed to the right step and tempo. We exchange partners. I'm a bit disappointed with that, but it doesn't take long for Prince Charming to be back after circling around with the other dancers.

We're laughing. I swear, it feels like we're children playing hopscotch. Then the childishness stops as Bryce passes beside me again. And I swear —no, I know—he looks into my eyes and gazes at my dress, checking me out.

"Bring the wreath down," Bryce says, still looking into my eyes. "Keep going, you guys. You're all doing great."

It's a lot of fun.

But I feel a little dizzy walking in circles. The torchlight streams by my eyes, a burning beam of red-yellow light. Then I hear the cracking of twigs and leaves rustling to my side.

I turn and am surprised to see a herd of deer in the brush. They're not far from the drummers. There's one really large stag with big antlers followed by a doe. Behind these deer is an adorable fawn. It's cute to see a deer family like that. I usually only see deer alone. But it's weird that no one in the group seems to notice the deer in the woods or even care. And it's also strange that the deer are so close to us.

Maddie bursts out into stupid laughter behind me. That makes me laugh too. Everybody's laughing and we're just having fun.

2

THE KISS

I close my eyes.

The laughter is like a pack of hyenas now. It seems to echo with the drums, only getting louder in my ears. The sound's surrounding me and making me feel dizzier. Everyone's acting so dumb, but we're all having so much fun doing it.

"Hold the hands of your partner," says Bryce between laughs.

Gladly. Because Bryce is my partner again. I grab Maddie's hand with my left and handsome's with my right. The streamers haven't been brought down to the base yet from the top of the pole, but now we're supposed to drop them and do some kind of dance around the branchless tree. My hands shake when the pole seems to wave like a vertical snake for a moment as the flower wreath slowly travels down the pole. That makes me feel even dizzier. Then we raise our hands high, and back down. It seems like we're following the vertical movement of the pole.

"You okay, Cadence?" Bryce asks, tugging my hand.

"Uh-huh." I nod. "Fine."

"You seemed a little unsteady."

Because I'm not fine. We stop and dip down a few more times. It's like we're bowing to it. And I'm only getting dizzier. My cheeks feel hot, not from embarrassment but from nausea. It dawns on me how impossible it is that the pole was waving at all. It's a stiff tree trunk. I'm beginning to feel sick enough to think there was something slipped into my drink. I look at Maddie to say something, but she's laughing too hard. And Bryce seems way too into staring at the pole for me to want to disturb him. But everything is blurring. Particularly the torchlight, which now seems like a red-yellow ball rather than a flame.

Cadence Hawthorne.

I hear someone say my name. Was it Bryce? Or do I just want it to be Bryce?

Cadence Hawthorne.

"Faster," Bryce says to the crowd. "Faster, Cadence."

Well, he said my name now.

I close my eyes again. It seems we're spinning too fast. It feels like I'm on one of those rides at the fair and we're twirling around and around, faster and faster. I hate those rides. I even hear screams in the far distance as if we're on a roller coaster. It feels like that. Like we're at the fair.

I open my eyes and the strangest thing is that my companions seem to be moving slower. But the pole, which is writhing upward more aggressively, seems to be growing taller.

Then I see flashes of light by the base of the pole. It's like someone is firing a firecracker. Then sparks crackle around the base.

Cadence Hawthorne.

"*Cernunnos!*" cries a girl in a black cloak. Her shriek makes me jump. She's standing across from me with her hood down, and I can't make out her face. I don't even remember seeing this girl before. Nor do I recognize her voice. "*Cernunnos!* Come forth and bless us with your presence, Cernunnos! Spring forth the Green Man. Witness virgins of fertility kneeling at your feet, providing offerings, before you join the May Goddess in handfasting. Bless us with your presence, Cernunnos, for a bountiful harvest and spring. Allow all our wishes to come true!"

"Cernunnos," echo all the students in black cloaks, including Bryce, beside me. "Cernunnos."

Cadence. Cernunnos.

Cadence. Cernunnos.

Cadence. Cernunnos.

The pole ignites in a burst of flame, and soon it's as bright as the bonfires near the Billington House. At first I think it's on purpose as part of this ceremony, but then I think that such a bright, bursting explosion came out of nowhere.

"Everyone," Tammy says, laughing. "Okay, everyone, let go of your partner's hands now and pick up a streamer. Pull the streamers all the way down. We've almost got it."

But I'm staring at this flaming trunk. It's really freaking me out. No one lit it. And the weird thing is Maddie and Bryce are just going about their business, picking up their streamers as if nothing happened. Everyone is. Tammy is acting like we're just finishing wrapping a tree. Am I the only one who thinks it's weird that our pole just burst aflame?

It starts to rain. There isn't a cloud in the starry sky. The water washes away the flame and smoke emanates from the base of the pole, misting everything around us, but the fire still burns strong.

I hear more rustling in the bushes. I expect it to be the family of deer. But it's only two deer now—one stag on top of a doe. The stag is making love to the doe.

My heart beats faster.

Maddie and Bryce are still picking up their streamers. How? Why is it taking so long? They seem frozen, with their hands touching the strips of paper on the ground.

"Maddie, what's wrong with..."

Beside my friend, in the shadow of a tree, is an older man. He is naked, but painted green, having sex with a girl lying on a bale of hay. The nearby torch is bright enough to shine over his bald green head and goatee. He's dirty with leaves all over his body. The lady is dark-skinned, with a red line of makeup over her eyes. And her face is powdered white. And she's wearing a garland of flowers, like Maddie's and mine. The drums are still beating in the background, now seemingly matching the thrusts of this Green Man over this girl. His green painted hand caresses her dark skin, squeezing her soft breasts and nipples. His ass tightens as he presses hard into her. Then he leans down and kisses her lips passionately.

Cernunnos. Cernunnos.
Cadence. Cadence. Cadence.

Maddie is holding her streamer in her hand, still frozen, just staring at what she wrote.

I turn to Bryce. He had dipped down on a knee, gazing at our burning pole. But now he's moving. Slowly. He casts his black cloak on the ground, and he's slowly unbuttoning his shirt. He seems hypnotized. I am embarrassed, but from the corner of my eye, I can't resist glancing at his bare chest. The rain drips along his pecs and ripped abs. He's cut as hell. My heart beats fast, I'm so excited. I have a desire to touch his wet skin. And pull my dress over my head.

I look back at Maddie. That's actually what she's doing. She's pulling her white dress up, exposing her black lace bra and panties. Now she's reaching back to unfasten her bra.

"Maddie," I exclaim, "don't! What are you doing? Stop!"

She removes her bra and stands there bare chested, staring at the pole. Then she pulls down her underwear.

I'm so dizzy. Everything is spinning now, faster and faster, even the surrounding forest, the ground and the moon too.

I see the stag and doe again. They're at it—faster. As I turn, trying to avert my eyes, I see the Green Man still fucking the Black girl. And everyone, all my dancing partners, are now taking their clothes off.

I close my eyes. I feel unsteady but, thankfully, there is only darkness. What's going on? I'm either drunk or poisoned.

Then I notice something weirder. My heart is thumping so hard, but I realize it's not fear. I'm not afraid. I realize that I like this. I feel wonderful. It's desire. Excitement is where I want to be. This is where I've always wanted to be. As odd as everything happening around me is, this weird naked evening ceremony feels absolutely right.

I touch my chest and run my hands along the white cotton dress and over my breasts. I press my left breast, and my heart is aching for me to touch myself—to pull up my dress and touch my naked chest. My eyes are still closed. I hear moaning. Groaning. I know what's continuing to my left, but I avert my eyes. I can't face it.

I force my eyes open and look past the pole. That's far worse. A naked couple is groping each other. I remember one wearing glasses, a jacket, and jeans and the girl beside him wearing a pretty light-blue summer dress—kind of like a blue version of the goddess Diana's dress, which

Maddie and I are wearing. Now the two of them are butt-naked making love. But they seemed like they didn't know each other when we arrived. Beside them, I see a burly nude guy with a thick beard squeezing a petite blonde's pale breast while he's holding her aloft in the air. His skin is painted red. He's bouncing her over him.

I close my eyes tight again. Part of me wants to run; the other is quaking with energy and desire.

"Are you okay, Cadence?" Bryce asks again softly.

I open my eyes. The pole isn't on fire. Bryce looks like Bryce. Then I look at the crowd, and they're all staring at me. I'm the only one not holding a streamer in my hand.

"You have to pick up your streamer," Tammy insists, squinting at me. "We have to finish."

Everyone looks "normal." Some are still wearing cloaks or flower garlands, but they're all wearing clothes. And they're all looking at me like I'm completely insane. Perhaps I am? Even the drummers stopped drumming.

"Sorry," I mutter, picking up my streamer with a shaky hand.

"Are you okay, babe?" Maddie whispers, leaning over.

"I don't know." But I force a smile at the group.

"Okay, guys," Tammy says again. "Let's finish. Grab your streamers and pull it down to the base of the pole."

The flower wreath sinks all the way to the ground as we circle it to the beat of the drum.

And there's no rain. The sky is clear. The pole isn't on fire. And no one is fucking anyone.

"That was fun, huh?" Bryce asks me. Then he squints his eyes and furrows his brow, touching my shoulder. "Are you sure you're doing okay?"

"I ... I just feel weird, that's all."

"Everyone kiss the person's cheek to your left," Tammy says with a laugh. Maddie's laughing too hard by my left side. "Now to your right."

That'd be Bryce. So, for the benefit of their ceremony and all, I gladly lean up on tippy-toes and pucker up. He expects a peck. It's not. I lean my whole body into him and press my lips and chest against him really hard. I force his mouth open and my tongue dances with his. My heart is thumping so hard and fast, and it's like the weirdness of the pole dance is happening all over again in his arms. But this time, it's with this handsome guy. I feel his hand press over my back and down to my bum, bringing me closer. Apparently, he desires me too. Again, I want to pull my dress off. I know that's crazy, but I'm that excited. Then my hand wanders over his face and brushes against the stubble on his cheeks. I want to take him, pull off his cloak, his shirt, and his pants, and gaze at his chest and stomach again with the rainwater dripping over his naked skin. I want to run my fingers down his cut abs. I want—

Everyone's laughing. *At me!*

Bryce backs up hesitantly from my lips and says with a nod, very sternly, "It was nice to meet you, Cadence."

"Uh... Yeah. For sure."

"Okay, everybody," Tammy says with a laugh. "Just a kiss. Now one more dip for the horned god of spring."

Bryce furrows his brow at me after we bow.

I've had enough. I feel like a complete idiot. I hightail it out of there, rushing back up the grassy hill, without looking back and without the company of my friend.

3

———————

BELTANE

"Nice kiss," Maddie says with a laugh, catching up to me. Then she tugs at my arm. "Just glad you didn't lay that on me. Damn. I mean, Bryce is hot and all, but... Hey! What's up? Where are you going?"

I want to get the fuck out of here. I'm rushing back up the grassy hill. I feel a mix of emotions, none of them good. Maybe it's because I was just hallucinating? I'm doubting my sanity. Maybe I have schizophrenia or something? You know that can develop around my age. The other thing is Bryce. I just met him. He seemed so nice and intelligent, someone I might want to really get to know, and I kissed him like a total whore.

"That was...fucking weird," I say, choked up, finally stopping. We're far enough from everyone else in the shadows of the trees. My best friend's face is still lit by the torchlight from the valley below. She's squinting and frowning. She looks concerned. That's sweet.

"Oh, god, Cadence," Maddie says, touching my shoulder. "What's the matter, babe? Tell me what happened?"

I'm going crazy.

"Kate, what the hell's the matter?" Maddie asks, searching my eyes.

I shake my head and pull away from her. "Why'd you take me here?" I ask. "I didn't like any of it."

"We were just having fun. It's May Day."

"No," I say, quickly shaking my head. "Somebody slipped something in my drink."

"What?" She laughs and that pisses me off more. "That's ridiculous. That was Bryce's mead."

"So? It was spiked."

"It wasn't," Maddie says, shaking her head. "It was made by Bryce."

"So? What about the deer? Did you see deer screwing in the bushes?"

Maddie opens her eyes wide.

"And what about dancing naked with everybody touching each other around a burning tree." After Maddie doesn't say anything, I add with a nod, "See. I was poisoned."

She's looking at me like I'm a total loon. But then she grows this infernal smirk and shakes her head. "Oh, Cadence, you had a vision."

"What?"

"A vision." She jumps into my arms with joyous laughter. "That is so cool! I didn't know it was possible. Tammy said that someone really in tune with wrapping the maypole might see something when celebrating, but I didn't really believe her. But it sounds totally like you—"

"*What do you mean, cool!*" I yank myself out of her grasp. "It wasn't a vision, it was your mead that was poisoned by that Bryce guy. I thought he was a good guy."

"I know. You seemed to like him when you kissed him."

"Shut up, Madison! It's not funny."

"Oh, Cadence. Tamms says that sometimes when you circle the maypole, the magic of Cernunnos can manifest. You weren't poisoned. Bryce would hurt himself before hurting you. Trust me. He is like the nicest guy in the world. He couldn't hurt anybody—too nice, honestly. He reminds me of you. The horned god sent you a vision. What'd you see? Nude, huh? How fun."

That's it. That's enough. I rush out of the woods back toward the Billington House with every intention to go back to our dormitory, because now I feel like I don't like my friend as much as I don't care for their stupid spring festival.

"Wait, Katie!"

She reaches for my arm again, but I swat her like the pest she is.

"Wait up! I've heard mostly that people have visions with special herbs and stuff." She's beside me, still seemingly excited about her *"vision"* shit. "You know, there are ceremonies that can bring them out. Like peyote in Navajo religious ceremonies, the Amazon tribes in Brazil have their own substance, or the use of Iboga in Africa. I just learned all about it in my anthropology class. But visions are spurred on by substances. I can't believe you had one without anything. That is so amazingly cool."

"Bryce's mead."

"No," she says with a laugh, grabbing for my arm again. But I'm not stopping. "Boy, you must have a lot of magic inside you, girl."

None of this makes me feel any better.

We approach the house and stop by rows of kids. I'm shocked by the number of students. Their stupid ceremony is starting. I squint at the two bright bonfires, seemingly brighter now. And the sight of fire bothers me, because it reminds me of the burning pole, or the fire I hallucinated around the pole.

Those same guys holding drums run by us. They all have green paint on their faces. I didn't notice their green paint before in the shadows of the trees.

"You know," Maddie infernally continues, "it could be our spinning. It's like whirling dervishes who get their sense of God by turning in circles. For all I know, it might not be the maypole at all. Maybe it was the spinning that brought magic out of you, Cadence. But I can't believe you saw something. That is so, so, so super cool. What'd you see? Tell me again. What was in your vision?"

"I saw an image of me killing you for taking me here." I fold my arms.

Maddie laughs joyfully. I'm not laughing. But then, I can't help but smile back at my best friend.

She hugs me in a half-embrace.

"It was really weird," I say with a nod. "Just...everyone was undressing."

"You're kidding. Was Bryce?"

I roll my eyes and look back at the two bonfires, where many people are holding torches.

I should head back to our dorm. I should maneuver around all the bodies and head home.

"Was he?" Maddie asks again, opening her eyes wider.

"I saw his chest."

"Ripped?"

"Just shut up."

"He works out. Too bad he's going on a study tour for the rest of the year. I think after your kiss, you two would be hitting it off for sure. It almost looked like you two were ready to pitch a home run, before all of us, right then and there."

"It's not funny, Maddie."

"Sure," she says, still laughing. "It kind of is. But you can't leave now. The ceremony's about to start. You don't want to miss this. Mom used to take me when I was little. It's really cool. Anyway, even if you want to leave, you won't get through these crowds until it's over."

Well, she's right about that. There's like five hundred people surrounding the fires now.

Dancing around the fire and even hopping over flames are people painted red. One of them I recognize as the red-painted topless girl that ran by us while I was studying. But there are many others. Weirdos with black bird beaks and feathers, a guy with a top hat, on stilts, wearing skeleton makeup, and many wearing druid cloaks like Tammy and Bryce. Some guys painted red are just wearing shorts. Many of them seem to be coming dangerously close to burning themselves over the fire. I wonder if some of them are students or if they came from elsewhere.

Behind me, I catch a guy in a black cloak but a really preppy button-down underneath walking up to me. It's Bryce. I'm not sure how he found us among all the bodies. I suppose we're still not far from the trail down to the maypole. I don't want to see him. I acted like an idiot. And seeing him reminds me of everything I just hallucinated.

"Are you okay, Cadence?" Bryce asks. "You were scaring me down there."

I was scaring you?

Bryce looks over at Maddie, and Maddie cups her hand by her lips and says with a smirk, "*Vision.*" Oddly, Bryce doesn't smile back. He seems to get very serious, almost concerned.

"It's really cool for you to have joined us," he says with a nod. "Thanks for coming, Cadence, Madison, and helping out with our pole."

"Did you put anything in my drink?" I snap, forward as hell.

But then I lose my scowl looking into his eyes. God, they're dreamy. I feel my heart racing again. He seems to get lost too, because it takes him a second to answer. Then he squints and looks down at the wild grass for a moment. He shakes his head and says, "I just made mead, Cadence."

"It was ... good. Thanks."

"Want some more?" he says offering his red cup.

"No!"

"All right," Bryce says slowly, opening his eyes wide.

"The pole was a lot of fun, Bryce," says Maddie. "Cadence has just never done that before."

We watch everyone getting ready for whatever the hell they're getting ready for. Bryce stands beside me, to my right, and puts his thumbs in his pockets and just watches too.

"Sorry," I say, cocking my head to Bryce. "It was fun. What are we waiting for now?"

The green drummers that rushed by us sit down with the group near the two huge fires. And others, beside them, in skimpy clothes are playing weird flutes.

"Beltane means fire," Bryce says. "It is May Day. This day is a huge deal for Hawthorne, having been celebrated for centuries. Many from all over the country, the world, come here to celebrate. Beltane marks the middle of spring, when the flowers are blooming at their greatest peak. The change of season is like the preceding Sabbat Ostara, but this one marks regrowth, renewal, and fertility."

Fertility. I get that.

"So we celebrate the May Queen marrying the Green Man," he continues, "The May Queen also represents the three witches of aging. She procreates, for the birth of the harvest, with the Green Man, or Cernunnos. That's what we're waiting for, Cadence: the arrival of the May Queen and the Green Man and their handfasting. When they have their handfasting, the ceremony is complete. We already missed a handfasting by the bonfires while we were circling the pole. That one was a real one."

"Handfasting?"

"A wedding, Katie," Maddie says.

"It's a pagan wedding," Bryce says. "You know. Instead of a ring, we believe in tying our hands. And then jumping the broom."

"Jumping the broom?" I raise my eyebrow. "Like a broomstick? That's stupid."

Maddie laughs. "Careful, Cadence. Bryce is really into this stuff."

"What you see isn't just show," Bryce says with a nod. "There's more to what you see than just fire or a tree trunk. There's meaning behind everything. You have to look further than your eyes, even further than the occult, or you'll miss out on the meaning. The meaning is what fascinates me. Take the fire..." He points and sips some of the mead he was poisoning me with earlier. "There are two great fires. Because in Celtic times you let your animals walk between two bonfires, representing their safe passage and purification from disease. The warmer climate meant the animals could roam free in your farm. But farmers were worried for the safety of their animals."

"So the fires aren't just two big flames blowing lots of smoke?" I ask.

"Minus the sarcasm, yes."

As I look again into those blue eyes dancing in the flames, I really don't give a shit about "Beltane" or animal safety. Or even my hallucination at the pole. I'm really into *him*. And his eyes. But then I look down, feeling humiliated again over our kiss.

"What am I going to do with you two," Maddie interjects with a chuckle. "I confiscated Cadence's notes, Bryce. We're here to have fun, not to be lectured. Kate, did you figure out yet that Bryce is a T.A.? And he likes all this pagan stuff. So Beltane is, like, his day. So don't make fun of it. It means you're laughing at him."

"Oh, I'm a history major," I say to Bryce, ignoring Maddie. He nods and drinks more of his mead. "What class do you teach, Bryce?"

"I'm Alondra's teaching assistant for her metaphysical history class. I also help run her honors program." He gestures to the cavalcade. "Here they come."

I reach for his red plastic cup. I mean, now that he's drinking it, it can't be spiked, right? So why not? He gladly hands it to me with a smile.

More fire comes our way as a whole group of black-robed people, their faces painted black, walk forward in two lines holding torches. Their black druid robes are similar to Bryce's. These black-clothed druids don't dance; they just walk to the two bonfires carrying fiery torches. Then guys and girls painted red leave their positions near the bonfires and dance their way to the torch procession.

"Why are those guys painted red, Bryce?" I ask my new favorite teaching assistant. I sip his sweet wine again.

"It represents fire," he says in my ear. But I can tell he doesn't want to teach anymore. He's looking intently at the performance.

Behind the black-cloaked druids comes another group of girls. They're all wearing white, and many have garlands on their heads, like me. They're younger girls and they remind me of flower girls at weddings. They're swaying back and forth, holding white wands. Finally, trailing them, come people dressed in weird bird costumes. The black beaks are creepy. Under the beaks, the bird people are holding flutes, playing in sync with the drums.

"Hi, Bryce," says a lady's voice behind me. "Glad I came in time."

I turn and my eyes bulge. I elbow Maddie really hard.

Standing beside Bryce is a woman I recognize, but I am unsure why the hell she's here. She's in a formal dress as black as Bryce's cloak. She's Dr. Alondra Johansen, the star history professor of Hawthorne University. Everyone knows and loves her classes. She teaches packed lecture halls and is the most popular teacher in the school.

"Did you decorate the maypole?" the professor asks Bryce.

Bryce nods. Then, oddly, he nods at me.

Dr. Johansen turns her gaze to Maddie and me. "Hi, Madison. Glad you could make the festivities."

"Hi, Dr. Johansen," says Maddie. "Cadence over here just wanted to study, but I talked her out of it."

Dr. Johansen smiles and nods to me. "There's a lot to study here. I'll expect your essay on Tuesday, Ms. Hawthorne. You can turn it in at the front office."

I turn to Maddie, surprised, and my best friend laughs. I hit her hard in the shoulder. I can't believe a teacher's here. But after her dumb joke, Dr. Johansen just watches the performance.

At orientation, I couldn't get over how damned nice Dr. Johansen was to everyone. She's always smiley. She's also very pretty. She's really pale but she has these emerald, almost too green, eyes. It's like they're not even real or something. And even in her formal work dress, she looks cute. I hope I'm cute when I'm old.

When I met her, you know, Dr. Johansen said, "Hi, Cadence."

"How do you know my name?" I asked.

She pointed at the name tag sticker on my sweater. I can be kinda absent-minded like that.

Anyway, it's right then that I gaze at my right hand. I almost drop the red plastic cup. I'm drinking underaged in front of a history professor!

Quickly, but nonchalantly, I hand my cup back to Bryce. He smiles and takes it back. I think he gets the hint. But then he's a T.A. So, technically, I'm drinking in front of him as well. But he gave me the drink? Right? So it's...okay? And so, I mean, I made out with...a teacher. A teaching assistant. Oh, god.

I use my newly free hands to grab my cellphone and quickly take random pictures of the fire ceremony.

The procession breaks off into two lines on either side of the fires. In the center, the red-painted weirdos keep hopping around. Then the raucousness gets really crazy. Anybody who has a flute or whistle blows like mad as a lady dressed in an elaborate red and white dress walks slowly down an aisle, along the wild grass, with a man. The man is, indeed, green. Like the red-painted fire boys and girls, the man is wearing leaves, and he is painted green. He has paint on top of his bald head too. And he has a sinister look. He kind of reminds me of the devil with his goatee and bald head. Then I recognize the May Goddess. It's Maddie's friend Tammy! She changed quick. Now I can see her urgency to get done with the maypole. Tammy's dark skin looks even darker against the red and white dress. But her face is powdered with white chalk and she has a red line of makeup over both eyes and ...

My skin crawls. I recognize this couple. This is the couple I saw having sex by the maypole in my vision. For some reason I didn't recognize, in my hallucination, the girl with the Green Man was Tammy. And now her face is made up the same way it was in my vision. And he's the same green guy.

I gasp. It's loud enough for everyone to turn. Including Dr. Johansen. Dr. Johansen furrows her brow, but then she folds her arms and smirks while turning back to the ceremony.

The fire dancers go crazy, their bodies bobbing and weaving around the couple as they approach the bonfires. Then the May Queen stands near the fire, and the Green Man bobs up and down around her too. He dances far slower because he's an old guy. The red dancers rush to the sides. Then it's just the Green Man circling the May Queen, as if he's laying ribbons around her, like we did with our maypole.

Then...everything stops. The drums stop.

The couple embraces. They embrace a little too close for my comfort because, like I told you, the Green Man is an old geezer. In fact, it's a bit lewd and reminds me of my kiss with Bryce. But as they hold each other, the crowd goes crazy with applause.

A group of people in those black druid cloaks walk up to them. They bind their hands with a strip of cloth. And they're married—ceremonially only, I hope.

There's more applause as the couple takes torches and joins their fire to both bonfires. Then the two of them walk between the two bonfires.

It's over.

Dr. Johansen turns to Bryce and hugs him. "Happy Beltane, Bryce. Blessed be."

"May you never thirst, High Priestess," Bryce says to her.

The professor turns to Maddie and me. "Happy Beltane, Cadence and Madison."

Uh... "Happy Beltane," I say. Then Dr. Johansen surprises me with a hug.

4

THE STRANGER

THE CROWDS RUSHING OUT OF THE YARD ARE CRAZY. MADDIE AND I DECIDE to stay put by the fires and let their numbers die down before returning to the dorms. Many walk through the forest to leave, but some pile into the frat house. It's like all of Hawthorne came to the ceremony. Now I know why my friend insisted so strongly that I attend. I would have been, like, a freak if I hadn't come—ironic in its own anomalous way. We disappointingly lose Bryce. Then we lose Professor Johansen.

So Maddie and I wait, just people watching. I think Maddie likes looking at the scantily clad guys painted red.

As the crowd thins, we head closer to the Billington House.

"I told you it'd be cool," Maddie says. "Last year was just as amazing. I remember my first ceremony, when I was a little girl."

"Your mom didn't want to come tonight?"

Maddie shakes her head.

"Well, your Aunt Jane is the funnest person I know, Maddie. I'm surprised she wasn't here."

Madison and Aunt Jane have lived near Hawthorne all their lives. That's why my friend knows so much about the ceremony. She told me it used to be held on Damson farm, but it was moved to the fraternity grounds a few years ago to be closer to campus. Most of the people attending are students anyway—except our history teacher, apparently. Her showing up is weird.

"She lets me go," Maddie says. "But she doesn't like the atmosphere since they moved it to the Billington House. Maybe it's the partying? She's not so hot that I'm here either. I tell you, Katie, there's a lot of pagan freaky stuff that happens the rest of the night that she warned me about." Maddie winks at me. "Speaking of that, maybe we should go find Bryce? You two seemed to be getting along pretty well again after sharing his spiked drink."

I'm not laughing.

We slow by a line of people heading toward the house. It's packed with bodies even more than ever.

"Everything was fun, Maddie. Except the pole. Thanks."

"Well, the pole decoration was a special treat 'cause of my friend Tamms. She's really starting to get into this ritual stuff. Not as much as Bryce, but really into it, you know."

"She was good in the performance. But I can't believe we saw Dr. Johansen."

Now we're by a bunch of white tents. They're serving food near the house. It's less smoky here and a bit darker, but the full moon is lighting the outdoor picnic tables. Of course, the bonfires still burn bright behind us.

"Katie, I told you before Alondra is the coolest professor—"

Maddie stops talking because Alondra Johansen is standing right in front of us. But neither of us is really looking at her; we're staring at who she's next to. She's beside a woman about Dr. Johansen's age, with dark brown skin, in a really weird forest-green druid cloak with a string of gold necklaces and bracelets. The stranger is bald and her eyebrows are shaved. They're both talking and serving themselves salad in paper plates at one of the tables.

"Who's that oddball in the green coat?" Maddie asks.

I shrug.

"Let's get something to eat and find out," she whispers with a wink. I know what she's interested in. Snooping.

My roommate grabs a paper plate and hands one to me as we're standing in line. Then we wait a few people behind Dr. Johansen and the stranger. Madison bends close to my ear and whispers, "Alondra's not only cool, Katie, she's mysterious. Don't you love it? She's like so full of—"

"Weirdness?"

We grab some hot dog buns and hotdogs. Then we wait for the line to end. With our single hot dogs, we follow the two ladies. The tables are surrounded by people. Even though it's late, the party's still raging. In fact, there's still heavy metal music blaring from the frat house.

There's a table open right next to Dr. Johansen and the stranger. Maddie sits beside me to "eat."

"You shall be a two-faced goddess," the green-cloaked woman says. "So says the wheel. I am sorry. It is too sad. I've come to give you my sisters' condolences from the Crescent City, as well as my own. We all feel sorry for you and pray for you. The wheel can be unfair."

"Don't lie, Kenosha," Alondra responds. "You think I deserve it." She forks some salad and eats a little. Then she flashes Kenosha a fake grin. "My hope is that I can make amends with all souls. Even Enora." She stops forking some carrots and looks at the stranger with her infamous smile. "Even you. There was a time when you wouldn't have minded this news so much."

"It was devastating. You are my friend."

"I know," Alondra gives a big sigh. "If only I could turn back time. I'd change so much, Kenosha. So much. Between you and—"

"Liam?"

"Sure." Alondra frowns. Then she slowly nods. "I was going to say Agnes, but him too. I haven't heard that name in a long time."

Maddie is as transfixed on the two of them as she was on the May Queen ceremony. She's such a gossiper. She's also really obvious. I mean, she has a plain hot dog on her plate with nothing on it and no drink.

"At least the job offer is something for you," Alondra says.

"I'm honored," Kenosha says. "I'll miss home, but..." She looks around and takes a deep breath. "These woods are wonderful. I've always loved Hawthorne the best. I'm so excited and grateful to you, Falconsong."

I bite into my barbequed hot dog. It's a bit charred but I feel stupid listening in on them. And Maddie's usually a chatter box. She's just snooping.

I get nervous because I swear I… In fact, no, I know I see the professor glance over. And even though she keeps talking to the green-cloaked oddball, she smiles for a second—it's that self-assured wry grin that she's so famous for. But she doesn't turn. That's Alondra. Maddie's right. She's mysterious.

"Too bad you missed the ceremony," Alondra says. She missed it? *Then why the hell is she wearing that weird green get-up!* "It seems better every year. This day was particularly full of magic."

"There was too much traffic," Kenosha says, forking some lettuce. "But I wouldn't be surprised if one of my sisters saw it. So many of us talk about it. Many of us come from home to see it. I'll find out for sure later."

"Anyway, you were right, Falconsong, you were right. I didn't believe in bad witches. Now I see that there is evil that wants to harm us. There is evil. I was wrong. More than that, I deceived you. For that—"

"It's over," Alondra says sternly. It surprises me. She looks angry. "Don't talk about it. In order to heal wounds, we must forget our mistakes. I'm over it, Kenosha. That's why I invited you here to Hawthorne University. You don't have to say another word. I'm just thrilled that you accepted."

Kenosha nods. "And I'm so happy that you chose me."

Alondra nods. "Welcome," she says with a smile. But her smile appears forced. She still seems angry. "Welcome to Hawthorne."

"I will seek herbs from the apothecary in Atlanta," Kenosha says with her mouth full of salad. "I will do what I can. I know you've asked for no intervention, but you're my friend. You've always been. I want to help you."

"As you wish. And now that you're here, I invite you to visit my home and attend whenever you want. My circle is your circle."

Then they fall silent. It's like that was all they wanted to say to each other. That's weird. They just eat their salads in complete silence.

A few students run past them, drunk. One even taps the professor and says hello. Dr. Alondra Johansen doesn't care that the student's inebriated. She laughs.

When Maddie and I have had our fill of our "dinner," I gesture for us to go. But Maddie yanks my hand and tells me to sit.

"What?" I hiss.

Maddie gestures to a tall man approaching Alondra. He's wearing a button-down and slacks. He's an older guy, but really cute. His brownish-red hair is combed perfectly. His eyes are dark and penetrating. And a large book is tucked under his arm. He seems really nice, but totally out of place at the Beltane party. He looks too "normal."

He nods to Kenosha. Kenosha, oddly, just waves and leaves them alone. But the really weird thing is Alondra's reaction. She lurches back with those emerald-green eyes wide in shock. She jumps up and embraces him. I catch a tear falling down her cheek. That tear makes me feel horrible for listening in. I'm hating Maddie for that. I feel like we're intruding.

I gesture to Maddie that we should leave, but she shakes her head more than ever.

"Oh, Lee, you came," Alondra says. "You came."

"I got the letter. God, Allie, I've missed you. I'm here for you, you know that. Always."

"You've always been," Alondra says, brushing his hair back from his eyes. "How long has it been?"

"You never stopped your worship of the backward pentacle."

"No," she says with a rueful smile. "And you could never accept both sides."

"But we still fight?" he asks. "Even now?"

She shakes her head and gestures for him to sit beside her.

Maddie leans over and whispers in my ear again. "Do you remember the ceremony? You know, the Green Man? He's with Alondra. So the question is, Katesy: Who the hell is that? They look a little bit too palsy-walsy to be friends, don't you think? Maybe she's having an affair? Or he's an old boyfriend? He's handsome enough."

"Shush," I say quietly. "Just shut up, okay?" Because Maddie is stupidly loud enough for them to hear her, even though she thinks she isn't. But she's also right. These two look like they know each other very well.

As the man sits down, he pushes the book before her. She runs her fingers along it. It looks very old.

"I hated you for hiding this," Alondra says with a nod. "It takes my bad fortune to finally get it? Not even when we were together was enough?"

"I suggested to Kenosha it was time. Agnes agreed that it was time to give it back to you."

"It was never theirs to take. It should have always been mine."

"I'm trusting you with it, Allie. I'm giving it back to you. I still don't agree with the things you did. But...with what's happened and with all those people you've helped, it's yours."

"It was never yours, Liam."

"Of course, I'm not giving it to you. Willow believes the descendant needs it. We expect you will hand it down. Is she here? You said, in a message last year, that she would be coming to school here."

"Yes, Lee. She's listening to us right now."

And Alondra turns and stares right at me. Maddie's eyes and mouth open wide. Then her hot dog falls out of her bun and plops on her paper plate.

"Girls, it's bad manners to eavesdrop," Alondra says.

"Sorry..." I stumble. "But...we weren't. We were just—"

"It's also evil to lie, Ms. Hawthorne," she says with a smile. "This is my good friend Liam. Liam, that over there is Madison Taylor. And her friend is Cadence Hawthorne."

"You've got to be kidding me?" he says, squinting at both of us. "They're sitting together? I don't believe it."

He gets up and walks over. He takes a knee beside Madison, which is cute as hell. "Madison, I remember you as a little girl. I'm sure you don't."

Maddie shakes her head staring at him.

"How's your mom? How's Jane?"

"Good." Maddie says, looking really stupid.

"She and I were once really good friends. Can you tell her Liam saw you at the festival? Tell her I said hi. Tell her how much I miss her. And say the words 'may you never thirst'."

Maddie nods.

"And you must be Ms. Hawthorne?" He turns to me. He's still on a knee, all chivalrous like. He sticks out his hand and I shake it. "Named after the town, I hear?"

"Sure," I say. "I guess."

Actually, I don't know much about why my name is from the town. Dad never told me. It's his side of the family. But I do think it might have helped me get accepted into the university.

"Are you one of the professors here?" I ask.

"No. I'm just visiting. It's a real pleasure and honor to meet you, Cadence Hawthorne."

Liam cocks his head back to Alondra. "And Bill? Is he here?"

"He's changing," she says. "You missed him in the ceremony?"

"Kenosha and I came late," Liam says, with a nod, standing up. "Give Bill my regards."

"It's a pleasure meeting you two," he says to us. Then he walks back to Alondra.

So now that we're found out, I'm expecting to return to the house and get my book back and study. But that wouldn't be Madison. She stubbornly leans over her plate, puts the hot dog back in its bun, and resumes eating her second dinner, which I know she really cares nothing about. And when I finally start getting up, she quickly touches my arm and shakes it as discreetly, but insistently, as she can.

"Kenosha's staying with you?" Alondra asks.

"No." Liam shakes his head. "I flew in alone. She and I met to come to the festival. And for me to give you back your book."

"Sit with me," Alondra says. "Talk with me. Don't go. You can stay over at my place tonight."

"You know I can't." He looks at me, and I think he's a little embarrassed. He seems quiet like me. "They remind me of that album you gave me once. Just like you and me, Allie. The one we spoke of. We were like that cover. You said it. An angel and her sister. A twin. Only, maybe we finally grew up, Alondra?"

She shrugs.

"You didn't have to ask me in the letter to come," Liam says, sitting down beside her again. "I don't blame you. There's nothing to mend between us. I'm always here for you. I never left. We just didn't believe in the same things."

"I'm trying to make amends with everyone before I go," she says with a nod.

"You never need to with me." He looks back at us hesitantly for a moment. Then he leans close to the professor and kisses her on the cheek. He speaks quietly, taking her hand, but I can still hear him. "I love you, Allie. Always. And I'm always here for you. You just need to call. Or see me anytime you want in the book. I wrote it all down there in your book."

"I love you, Lee," she whispers, but it sounds really pained.

He doesn't leave. Alondra doesn't let him. She seems to cling to his wrist.

Maddie and I do. I tug Maddie really hard. At first, she doesn't budge, so I hit her on the shoulder.

I mean, I still can't help but glance back myself. And even as I do, they're like two lovers sitting quietly at the table, ignoring the raucousness around them and just enjoying each other's company. And I don't know why, but they look so happy together. And somehow, that makes me feel very sad.

5

GOTHIC

Maddie and I are lying on blankets, wearing matching dark shades, on a grassy knoll on campus. It's a favorite spot to study or just lounge during a warm Sunday morning like today. It's particularly nice, with wisps of white clouds amid a lovely azure sky. If you look up the grassy hill, you can see our library and other modern buildings from central campus. The library's pretty cool. It's been remodeled and is like five stories high.

"What'd you mean he's going on a study tour?" I ask.

"A study tour, Katesy," she says, "means Bryce is traveling to study for his mentor, Dr. Johansen. See, Hawthorne is so boring that we don't have much to study, 'cept trees. So our history department is sponsoring a trip with Dr. Johansen to places all over the country."

"I know what a study tour is."

"Okay, smarty pants. Then..." She turns to her side and looks at me behind her shades. "Why'd you ask me?"

"What's he studying?"

"Witchcraft."

"Of course."

"He's stopping in Salem and all sorts of black-magic spots: East Hampton—though that might be for fun, I don't know—and then New

Orleans. He's going with a few other teaching assistants and students from Dr. Johansen's class this summer. And, real sorry to tell you this, Kate, but I hear he won't be back until after late September or October of our fall semester. But you're enrolling with me in his class, right?"

I nod.

Then I say, "witchcraft," lifting my eyebrow. I shake my head. "Some of your friends even dress like witches with all that goth makeup, Maddie. Just you better not start. Your goth friends are real weirdos."

"Sure, Cadence," Maddie says, laughing and lying back down on her back. "They're all actually pretty nice. You liked Tammy, right?"

"She's very nice."

"Tell me, what'd you get on your Ancient Civ test?"

"I got an A."

"'Course, you did, you bookworm. And you were worried about Beltane messing up your grades."

"It almost did after that T.A. going on a witch quest roofied me."

"He didn't, Cadence."

I close my eyes, enjoying the sound of leaves rustling gently in the wind. There are students chatting in the distance up by the campus coffee house. It's nice to just relax on the weekend, you know.

I try to think of nothing. But then I see an image of Bryce looking down into my eyes. He was really dreamy.

All summer. I have to wait all summer to see him again. Oh well.

"You doing okay now?" Maddie asks. "You're not seeing anything strange anymore, I hope?"

"Nope. Only when drinking mead."

"Well, it seemed like you liked him."

"Bryce was nice too."

We both laugh.

"A witch quest, huh?" I ask. "That's such a weird thing to study for the summer. God, Maddie, that's so weird. Well, you better not leave me and join them."

Maddie rolls on her side again and tips her shades down showing me her eyes. She laughs. I don't join her. I'm horrified. Behind her shades, she's been hiding thick black goth eyeshadow. She looks totally goth.

"Oh, Maddie!" I snap, shaking my head in disapproval. "Maddie! What are you doing?"

She just laughs.

"Don't tell me you're going with them this summer without me?"

"I'd never leave you, Cadence." Maddie shakes her head. "We're besties for life, remember? And I told you, we're gonna stay at my house at Aunt Jane's. We're gonna have so much fun." Then she adds, with a giggle, "Say, how about right now we head back to our dorm and I color your eyelids dark too?"

THE END

SAMHAIN WITCH

1

THE HAWTHORNE COVEN

FIRE CRACKLES, DANCING BEFORE MY EYES AND WARMING MY FACE. IT LIGHTS the cold evening air, so peaceful that it's more reminiscent of a candle than a bonfire. I absolutely love it. Tonight, the night before Halloween, it feels nice outside. Tranquil.

I'm holding my hubby Bryce's hand on my right and my friend Frida's on my left. The witches—all fourteen of us—are sitting around in black cloaks, hoods off, on white plastic chairs surrounding the fiery flame. Diana casts a full moon tonight, and the twinkly stars are out. Here in our rural college town of Hawthorne, the sky is always clear and the night sky is beautiful. I'm a little cold, but that's okay. I take a deep breath, so happy to be in the company of friends. Halloween is my favorite time of the year, you know.

"Yatu."

"Yatu," they answer. *Yatu* means hello.

"Lux alba," I say with a smile. "As heat turns to cold, leaves change from green to red and brown, as Astraeus awaits the rise of the Sun King, we reflect on lives lost. Our friends and family who've passed into the Summerland. Maybe a close loved one. Cousins, friends. Dogs, cats—" I turn to two of our new recruits, Jessica and Chandra. "Even goldfish." They laugh. They look nervous—all four of our new recruits do, still acclimating to our witchy ways.

"Whatever souls who you loved who have left you, you may celebrate their passing tonight. Tomorrow, when we hold the festival here, it won't be quiet like tonight. People will be doing what they've done for centuries, wearing masks, dancing, just having fun. In centuries past, the costumes were meant to frighten away evil spirits during this time when the veil between life and death is thin. Tomorrow, it will be done in our backyard for celebration. But let us not forget, sisters, the feelings we hold together right now. As I draw down the moon, do not forget the peace in our circle, my Hawthorne coven."

"That's so nice, Katie," says Frida in her Brazilian accent. She nods with her eyes closed.

I smile and nod too. Then I stand up. Everyone stands with me.

"Blessed be the day that the circle is brought together. Blessed be the coven under our gods Gaia, Selene, and Astraeus. Tomorrow is Samhain. In this season, let none of us thirst. Blessed be."

I stand and close my eyes, but I feel eyes watching me. Then I meditate on nothing but the peace under Selene, our full moon, slowly raising my arms and imagining holding the moon in my hands. With it, I will the fire to grow, its flame rising twice as high over us. A couple of witches gasp, seeing my fire magic. I'm guessing that's our newbies this year.

"Now let us turn our attention to Blackbird."

And we all sit back down to listen to my best friend, Madison, across the bonfire.

"Thank you, High Priestess Katesy," Maddie says. We laugh. "Listen guys, tomorrow, because of Kates and Bryce over here, we're gonna have so much fun! The history teachers are holding a Halloween party at their house! Alondra's old house. 'Cause you all know what happened to the Billington House last year."

"It was terrible," says Frida.

"Yeah. Right, Frida, but tomorrow, you guys are all gonna help Windstorm over there make Falconsong's old place the Samhain capital of the world! Because Cadence has cold feet. She's nervous over everything."

"I'm not," I object.

"You kind of are, sis," says Damie, my brother, sitting beside Madison.

My brother Damien's here, you know, because Maddie's here. He's going out with my best friend. Let's not talk about that.

"I just want the party to turn out okay, guys," I say.

"It will, babe," says Bryce. "Don't worry." And he squeezes my hand tightly with a smile. That's so cute.

"Aha, so here's the idea," Maddie continues with a nod. "We all meet at like six in the morning to start preparing. I know we're witches, so mornings suck, but we've gotta get up real early tomorrow to get all our shit together. Helen's gonna bring a lot of scary party favors. You know, we're gonna have to bob for apples—like in the classic Charlie Brown special—have a pumpkin carving contest and a costume contest, and caramel apples too. We'll clear the logs from our bonfire and get planks together to set up a stage."

"I thought we were going to have a band?" asks shy Helen. "Didn't Greg know a band that was going to play, Frida? That's what Katie wanted to do."

"Aha," Maddie replies. "That too, dope. But after music we'll all be voting for the best costumes."

"I'm not wearing a costume," says Mandy disdainfully. "Halloween parties are disrespectful to witches. We should be honoring the dead, displaying food and drink as sacrifices to Hecate, perhaps cake and wine as offerings. Not roaming around drunk with stupid jocks in white sheets."

"Katie wants us all to wear our black cloaks, Mandy," Frida objects. She turns to me. "It's really not a costume. Right, Cadence?"

"Best time to wear them, I figured," I say with a shrug.

"And candy corn," adds Maddie with a nod. "And plastic skulls and fake cauldrons and lots of cobwebs. Yeah, look, don't be such a goddamn downer, Mandy, 'kay? Jeesh. Let's try to have a little fun."

"We can have fun and still be witches," Mandy says.

"Phooey, Mandy. Phooey. Just...lighten up. Okay? Or I'll throw a white sheet over your head." We laugh again. "Anyway, I also got pumpkins and black plastic crows. A ton of holiday-shit shopping downtown in Atlanta yesterday."

"I'll bring a metal tub," says Josie. "It's totally huge and perfect for apples, guys. And I thought we could bake pumpkin pie."

"I'll get more apples," Bryce chimes in.

"What should we use for water?" asks Natasha. "Just the hose? The whole thing doesn't seem very hygienic."

"Now you're sounding like Mandy," says Jessica.

Well, Natasha and Mandy are best friends, and they always like to act like total downers. Mandy folds her arms and scowls at Jessica under the light of the flickering flames. With her dark eye makeup and lipstick, she looks like a real witch. She can be so mean, but somehow her anger tonight makes us all laugh. We're just in that good a mood. Mandy shakes her head but cracks a smile.

My mind drifts off. I mean, everybody in the group is having so much fun, and I adore that, but I'm worried. I know it's silly, but I've felt the same way all year.

If Alondra were alive, she would be in charge of my circle. And she would be running Bryce's metaphysical history class. Yeah, this year Bryce and I, with the help of the dean, are reviving Alondra's old history class. It used to be the most popular class here at Hawthorne U. And I'm Bryce's graduate teaching assistant. As incredible as it is to be working with my hubby, the stress of trying to live up to my former teacher is driving us batty. (Couldn't resist. I know *batty* is corny, but, hey, it's Halloween).

My nervous thoughts are interrupted by the sound of an owl. But I sense that the owl's hoot is miles from us, in a shadowed valley amidst our thick forest, perched on a tree over a stream. I see the owl in my mind's eye. The sound of her hoot sends a field mouse scurrying directly under her in the thick brush. Having a vision frightens me, because visions are triggered by threats or spells.

"And when Satan comes back to take Stingy Jack's life," Bryce is saying. I turn to my right and realize he's teaching. We're not just witches, you know, we're running an honors class. "He asked that, if Jack was to die, he'd have one last beer before death."

"That's something you'd do, Bryce," quips Natasha. The group laughs.

"Yeah, well, Jack and Satan get drunk. Then Satan says it's time for Jack to be taken down under the earth. But before Lucifer can take good ole Jack down, Jack asks that Satan turn himself into a gold coin to trick the bartender into thinking he paid and then for Satan to change him back when the bartender isn't looking. Satan is so impressed by the deception that he agrees. He turns himself into a coin. Then Jack tricks Satan by stuffing him inside his pocket, along with a cross."

There's a black bird circling overhead, amidst moonlit clouds, above the owl. The mouse is deep under the leaves, shaking.

"Years go by and somehow Satan gets freed. Satan tells Jack that it's time, once again, to be sent to hell. Jack says, 'Okay, I'll go down to hell if you grab me an apple from an apple tree.' Satan agrees. I don't know why." A few of us laugh. "Then when Satan's up in the tree, Jack carves a cross on the trunk with a knife. Satan is trapped. He lights the leaves on fire in a rage, shouts to the heavens, and goes batty. (Guess now Bryce likes that word). But he can't get down from the tree because of the cross. So Jack makes a deal with Satan to swear to never send him to hell if Jack scratches out the cross."

I think I recognize the black bird, now flickering in the moonlight as it hovers over the water, as a raven. In my mind's eye, I can see the stream and surrounding trees below her. Although it's dark, through the bird's eye it's clear enough. Not only does the bird see the owl; she sees the mouse hiding under a bush.

Libera Amica. Amica. Amica. Libera.

My hands clench tightly, and my fear turns to anger. *Amica* is the name for Enora's animal totem. That bitch used to change into a bird named Amica to trick me. For so long, Enora acted like my friend, Amica, when all along she was plotting to hurt me. Somehow I feel her presence in that black bird. She's here and she's free—free to hurt us.

"Time passes and finally, for a third time," Bryce says, "Stingy Jack is told he must die. So he climbs to heaven, and up there God weighs his deeds. As you can imagine, Jack is not the most righteous man—he's clever and evil, able to trick Satan himself, and, of course, *stingy*. So God tells Jack he has to descend to hell. But Stingy Jack can't descend because he bargained with Satan to ensure that he'd never go there. So Jack's stuck on Earth. And that's why townsfolk learned to use this guy to keep spirits from entering their homes—using a lantern. A jack o' lantern."

"*Ecce spiritus vester*," I say with a nod. "*Libera Amica. Vade retro. Vade retro Enora.*"

"And..." Bryce hesitates and turns to stare at me. "That's why we carve...pumpkins."

But my words have taken everyone's attention away from Bryce's pumpkin carving story.

"What's wrong?" asks Maddie, almost in a whisper.

"Yeah, why'd you say that, Katie?" asks Frida.

My eyes open wide. "I don't know." I quickly shake my head.

"You said 'Enora,'" adds Natasha. "Is Enora here?"

Everyone's creeped out.

I jump when Maddie points to something or someone behind me. Enora? But before I turn, I hear the stranger. She's crying behind me.

Shadowed before the dim light from the windows of my house, a middle-aged, very pale-skinned woman is on her knees wiping tears with a sleeve of her white blouse. She also has on white pants. Amidst all my witches' black cloaks and black makeup, her face looks very white, like porcelain white, with light gray eyes.

"Sorry, I didn't know where to turn," she says, wiping her eyes and shaking her head. "I'm looking for the Hawthorne Witch. I guess I lost it when I didn't see her here in your circle."

"You just said 'Enora,' Cadence," Bryce reminds me.

But this pale stranger isn't Enora. She has a thick Southern accent, like Natasha and Mandy, who are now standing right beside me.

"Ma'am, this meeting is private," says Natasha. "So is the yard. You need to leave."

"Sorry," the stranger replies, "but no one answered the door, so I wandered through the side yard. Y'all..." She smiles. "Are witches, right?

I'm looking for Alondra. Alondra Billington. Is she here? The Hawthorne Witch? I lost control of myself when I realized she might not be. My family needs her help."

"Alondra's left us," I say. The stranger looks like she's going to fall apart again. "But she was my teacher and friend."

"Alondra Billington helped rid my house of ghosts years ago, but now they're back. They appear every year the day following Halloween. I don't know what to do. I've had supernatural experts check the house. One even taped the phenomena. There's loads of weird stuff already happening this week. Yesterday everything was thrown off our kitchen table while we were eating lunch. Then the cabinet doors started opening and closing by themselves. And then windows shattered. I'm so dreading Sunday. Every year, the day after Halloween, ghosts attack my house. And—" She holds back tears again. "I'm most worried for dear, sweet Kathy. I don't know how much more of this a mom can take."

"This is a private meeting," Mandy says again, walking between us. "You have to leave."

"Stop it, Mandy," I say, raising my palm. "She needs our help."

"But she has no right to be here during our Sabbath, High Priestess."

My whole coven is standing behind me. And the weirdest thing is all these black-cloaked figures don't seem to faze the stranger at all.

"Please," the stranger says, raising a hand. "I'll do anything. Tomorrow will be such a nightmare if you don't help poor Kathy. Alondra knew. She used to cast shield spells every year after Mabon to prepare for Samhain. Last year, we lost that protection. Now that you say she's left, I see why. But you're witches, right? Perhaps you can come to the house in Geneva tomorrow and help us."

"Geneva, Switzerland?" asks Maddie, now beside me.

"No, Geneva Forest Alabama," she says with a chuckle. "It's close to here. Can you come?" She shakes her head quickly. "Poor Kathy's desperate. I told Mom she should have sold the house years ago. She tried, but the haunting stories stuck. Now, with recent events, there's no way we will ever sell the place. We don't have the money to move, you see."

"But I don't know how to get rid of spirits, Winona," I say. "I'm not Alondra. She never taught me or any of us how to do that."

"What did you just say? What name did you call me?" And she stares, opening those creepy eyes. Her eyes seem glassy, almost unreal.

"Allie told me."

"Allie, Cadence?" asks Bryce, lifting a brow. "Who's Allie?"

I shake my head hard. I'm in a trance again.

Everything turns dark. The black bird dives for the mouse. I think I'm perched on the tree watching. Am I seeing this through the owl's eyes? I'm not sure. As the raven snatches the mouse in its beak, a huge shadow leaps from the bushes and swallows the bird whole.

"You're the Hawthorne Witch," the stranger says, waking me from my vision with her creepy eyes. She smiles and that looks even creepier. "She called you High Priestess. Please. Please help us, Hawthorne Witch. If Alondra is gone, you can help me now. Please. You must help me."

I look up at the full moon. The moonlight is tranquil. But I don't feel tranquil. If I'm in a trance, I should feel Hecate's power. Not tonight. I'm afraid.

"It's Halloween," I say, shaking my head again, as if trying to shake off my fear. "Winona, maybe your hauntings happen at the turn of the season. For us, this day is the start of the pentacle. The best time to see the dead among the living. It's one of our most sacred times of the year."

"I know. I'm a witch too."

"But Alondra never taught me necromancy. I wouldn't know how to get rid of your ghosts. Or cast a spell to stop this."

"Please," Winona says, grabbing both my hands. Her hands are ice cold. "Oh, please try! At least try. For poor dear Kathy. Please just come to the house on the first day of the new year under Selene. You must at least try to see if you can help me."

And then she falls apart again. Frida rushes over and puts an arm around her. We all stand over the poor woman as she's shaking, on her knees, in tears.

2

PUKA

Shadows of tree trunks blur past me as I rush by. I'm bobbing up and down, riding at terrific speed. Wind rushes through my long hair and along my cheeks. I'm thrown side to side, my legs clinging tightly to the horse, and I'm afraid I might be bucked off. When I enter a grassy clearing under the full moon, I just race faster. I don't know how I'm here. I don't even know how to ride a horse! The horse pants and I swear I see smoke from his nostrils as he rears his head back. Half of me is aware, the other feels drowsy. Moonlight occasionally peeps from the shadows in the valley below, but it's dark. Honestly, half of me doesn't feel like I'm with you at all right now.

Ecce spiritus vester. Amica. Amica. Vade retro Enora.

In a dark living room a woman is sleeping under her couch. I'm not sure why she's chosen to sleep curled up on the carpet. The couch is empty except for a pillow and blanket. Another girl is in a corner of the room, but it's so dark that I can't make out who it is. I recognize the woman under the couch: Winona. A sliding glass window is shaking in the wind, and the shadows of trees are swaying in the darkness outside as rain splashes against the glass. But it's so dark that the window is the only thing dimly lighting the room. Something pulls me away from the living room. I don't know why, but I'm beckoned to walk to a stairway. As I walk up the steps, I feel fear. It's like some primal fear.

Children's laughter echoes around me.

I turn my head, but I'm too far up now to see the living room downstairs. I see a cloud of red smoke. There's a smell, something I've smelled before: cinnamon, sulfur, and sandalwood. The last time I smelled that was in the depths of Enora's underground lair.

Sanctus, sanctus, exitus.

~

I look down. My bare, muddy legs are straddling a black horse. But, thankfully, my horse isn't racing anymore; he's slowly trotting. I'm close to a trickling stream under the bright moonlight. I'm naked.

I clench my fists tightly, stabbing my palms with my fingernails, trying to awaken from this dream.

Sanctus, sanctus, Hawthorne.

~

My eyes open to a scream. Grunting. My horse? No. Something growls. It doesn't sound like any animal I've ever heard. The red mist is gone. The wall beside the stairs shakes. I feel unsteady. There's a ripping sound along the walls, as if the wall is being torn apart. I nearly fall as the steps beneath me swerve back and forth.

"Stop it, Melanie! Stop it! They're trying to help you!"

"Winona pushed me. She pushed me, Momma. She pushed me down the stairs!"

~

My horse is trotting over water. I look up at the full moon. The bright white orb is still among fast-moving wisps of clouds. It's beautiful. It's a small respite of peace. The moonlight, reflecting over the water and flickering along leaves and tree trunks, is nearly as bright as sunlight.

"Blessed Diana," I whisper, "please awaken me from this dream."

A red sun appears beside the moon. I realize this is impossible, but somehow the sun has appeared at midnight, next to the full moon.

Lux alba.

White light brightens everything. I squint from the blinding light.

"Alondra," I whisper, "please, teacher, help me awaken from this wandering. Help me wake up from this nightmare. Show me the way."

I close my eyes tight.

Spiritus. Venite foras. Spiritus. Spiritus. Venite foras.

In a small dark room, clothes, a large doll, some tennis balls, and pieces and papers from a board game are strewn on the floor. Most odd, two beds and a rocking chair are stacked at the side of the room. In the center of this room is a pitch-black orb. I recognize the onyx orb as a person in a black witch cloak. This is a witch in a meditative pose. It can stir great magic. The woman in the orb position keeps chanting, "*Spiritus. Venite foras.*" It's Alondra's voice.

The witch looks up. But...is it Alondra? A girl younger than me is wearing our hooded black cloak.

"What can I do to expel the ghost?"

"Windstorm," Alondra says, tears rushing down her face. And her green eyes look deeply into mine. "Windstorm. This I breathe. Hawthorne Witch. Wait for the next one. And leave me, Lee. It's me. It's me."

Alondra lays her head in her arms and weeps. I feel like crying too. I don't know why, but it seems like Alondra's lost everything and I'm so sad.

When she calms herself, she slowly raises a shaky outstretched arm and points to the wall.

Against the dimly lit wall, I see a dark-skinned bald witch wearing a cloak, like our black cloaks, but this one is forest green. This witch is pinned upside down, as if nailed to the wall, in the shape of an X. I recognize her face. It's Kenosha, the dean of our school. She is a powerful witch but, just like Alondra, Kenosha looks much younger than I've seen her before. Kenosha seems to be in pain as she desperately tries to get off the wall.

There are screams. It's the little girls again, but this time they're not laughing—they're panicked.

Everything grows dark.

~

"Cadence! Cadence!" I fight with all my might against the arms grabbing me. I feel like Kenosha, stuck on the wall. "Cadence! Wake up, Cadence! Wake up!" But it is Bryce's voice.

"*Lux alba!*" I yell.

My eyes open to Bryce holding me by the shoulders, his eyes searching my face in the moonlight. He looks so worried. I look down and see he's in a T-shirt and pajamas. But the weirdest thing is both of us are standing in water in a shallow brook. We're outside. It's dark, but it's not too dark with the full moon overhead.

"Oh, Cadence, what's happening?"

"I'm sad." And I start crying. It's stupid, but I can't help it. I keep thinking of Alondra. She was so upset. It's like her whole world had fallen apart before me, and I think her spirit wanted me to see that.

He hugs me and wipes tears from my eyes. I squeeze him tightly. I felt so cold after walking through that dark house, but now Bryce's warmth means everything to me.

"A wandering?" he whispers in my ear. "A wandering, baby? Why? What's wrong? Was it Enora?"

"No," I say, shaking my head. "Not Enora. Alondra. I saw a vision of her while riding a black horse. She was crying, Bryce. I think it was Alondra's past, and her spirit put me in this wandering to show me. She was so sad, so upset, in Winona's house, as if everything was over for her. It was horrible. It makes me so sad."

"Something threw you into a trance in bed," Bryce says with a nod. "You just got up and walked outside."

"Alondra's telling me to go to Winona's house tomorrow," I say. "I've been remembering something about Winona in *Broomstick* since she came by the house yesterday. There's something about her, something that was so vital to Alondra and, now, is important to all of us. But what's weird is Alondra pointed to Kenosha as if Kenosha was the problem. I mean, I don't like Kenosha, but I don't think she's bad. Is she? I...I don't know, Bryce, what Alondra was trying to tell us."

"God, babe, who cares? Let's just go home. You went so far."

But everything's clear. Too clear now. I look about me at the shallow stream, shimmering under moonlight. My magic has made everything crystal clear. But with all the power gleaned from being in a trance, how was I still feeling threatened?

I'm shaking. It's not from sadness or fear; it's because the water's frigid. It's then that I realize that I might be shivering not only from the "coldness" of Winona's house, but from the literal coldness of the icy water at my feet—because I'm standing naked, barefoot in this running brook.

My lips land softly on Bryce's lips. I know, it's weird, but I feel like he's my refuge and I just want to kiss him. The scent of him mixed with the ground is amazing. He's my escape from the cold I've been feeling ever since yesterday's Sabbath. My fingers wander over his short hair, while the other hand wanders under his shirt, tracing his rock-hard abs and the thin hair on his chest. And we just kiss. And it's nice. He's warm. My free hand wanders under his pajama pants, and...

"Cadence! You're scaring me. It's the middle of the night and we're in the middle of the forest!"

When in a witch wandering, it's not only my magic I feel, but a primal feral desire. I'm in touch with the forest and my most base instinct comes out. And that must be drawing me close to the love of my life right now.

"Warm me, Bryce," I say, hugging him again.

He takes off his shirt and drapes it over me.

That's not exactly what I had in mind. But it's not so bad because now I see his ripped abs and back under the moonlight. He tries to lead me out of the water by taking my hand, but I refuse to go.

"Take me," I say, shaking my head. "I want you. Remember our first time in the forest? Take your witch wife under blessed Selene deep in the forest tonight."

I readjust in his grasp and hear the water clapping at my feet. That reminds me of sex. Then I see flashes of visions of Bryce's well-built physique, his strong arms, his naked butt, his fingers gliding along my skin.

"Cadence," he says, backing up again with a nervous chuckle, "you're not yourself. You said you rode a black horse? Like a Puka?"

"*A whata?*"

"A Puka? You rode a black horse? In Ireland during Samhain, townsfolk were known to take rides on Pukas. They're black spirit tricksters. Sometimes they appear in the form of a horse. Other times they look more like goblins. And other times, they can talk."

"Okay, professor. So?"

"This might not be from Alondra's ghost. It could be a bad spirit telling you to go to Alabama tomorrow. Alondra told me she rode a Puka during Samhain once. They're mysterious spirits, shadowed from the spirit world, and they're usually up to no good."

"Did Alondra ride naked?"

My back is thrown hard against a tree trunk. Is it Bryce's desire? It must be. "You're putting a spell on me," he breathes. I am? What about him? He runs his fingers along the curves of my breasts and hips. His skin is moist from the mist. Then he lifts my whole body in his strong arms. The bark is hard and cuts a little against my back and ass. The sex is rough, like the bark against my skin, like my bare-chested, ripped man, but that's okay. It feels wonderful. I touch his thin beard, run my hand across his cheek, and enter his mouth again with my tongue. And we just French kiss, and it's so wonderful being so close to him in the woods.

"Cadence, stop it!"

He backs away from my lips. I look down and I'm not against a tree. I'm still standing beside him in the water. Wait... How?... We haven't even moved. I must still be in a trance.

"We have to go home, Cadence," he says.

"Sorry," I manage despite my witchy desire.

"Do you even know where you left your clothes?"

"Nuh-uh."

"Are you still sad?"

"Not with you here with me, Bryce."

"Are we in danger?"

"Yes," I say, meeting his gaze for a moment with a giggle, "you are. From me."

He doesn't respond. He doesn't even laugh. He just tugs my hand, leading me over to some thick bushes. I think he's afraid of saying something to trigger me. Is he too late? Probably. I told you, taking his shirt off was not a good move. I keep staring at his bare back as he leads me out of the water and onto the dirt and mud.

"It's such a lovely night under the full moon. You sure you don't want to make mad love to your witch wife, Bryce?"

"Maybe at home after you shower."

Boy, that was the wrong thing to say.

"We'll never make it," I say.

3

GHOST STORIES

I hear these strange words recited behind me as I'm lugging a huge orange pumpkin to our makeshift wooden stage in my backyard. I recognize the voice and nearly drop the large pumpkin on my foot. Then I quickly heave the pumpkin onto the stage near some decorative cornstalks and turn around.

"Mira!"

"Hi, Cadence," Mira says, waving a hand.

"Hi, Cadence," echoes a young, lanky blonde holding her hand. Mira's wearing a very long black dress with thick dark makeup. Courtney's in a skimpy black T-shirt and shorts, and her paleness contrasts with the black clothes. But, of course, she's got goth makeup on her face too.

Mira puts her arms around me. Then Courtney hugs me too.

"I couldn't miss little Katie's party," Mira says to me with a grin. Then she laughs, shaking her head. "Only you would wear designer sunglasses with a black witch cloak, Cadence. But it's cute. It's something Alondra would do."

"I thought you guys were busy this weekend?" I say, trying to ignore her typical insult.

"Yeah, well, Courtney fucked it all up. She forgot to send the invites."

"I didn't, Meer."

"You did. But that's okay. Like I told you, I want to watch Katie's attempt at running a Billington House party. A substitute Hawthorne Halloween celebration."

"It's not a substitute. I just thought students would enjoy celebrating in another classic estate at Hawthorne."

"Yeah," Mira says. She watches Maddie tying corn husks to the patio columns. "But no student is going to have fun at a professor's house. Why do you think Alondra never held parties for students here? And Samhain isn't all about vampiresses or zombies being cute for a first crush, knocking on doors saying trick or treat, and cutting holes in pumpkins. It's about celebrating the turn of seasons. Our new year to honor the dead."

"Then why are we here, Meer?" says Courtney in a huff, putting her hands on her waist. "You're being a total bitch to Cadence."

"Shut up, Courtney," Mira says with a chuckle. "That's *our* tradition together. But hate to say it, Cadence, I really think no one's gonna come to this backyard. Certainly not students to drink."

"No beer, Meer?" asks Courtney, pouting.

"Mira!" cries Maddie, running over. She scoops Mira up in her arms and they laugh. Then Maddie hugs Courtney. "I thought you two were going to stay in Atlanta?"

"Nope," Mira answers. "Hawthorne this Halloween. Gilda's coming later too."

"So what's the plan, Maddie, bobbing for apples?" teases Courtney.

"Yep," Maddie says with a grimace.

Mira rolls her eyes.

But then it's as if Mira never left. Mira's helping Frida and Josie carry pumpkins to the stage with me. Bryce isn't back yet. He drove into Flintwood to get more decorations for the inside of the house. But Natasha and Mandy are raking leaves on my wild grass. Helen and Jessica are out hanging webs and orange and brown streamers over our white wooden patio. Though it's chilly, it's a lovely clear blue sky. That's why I'm wearing the sunglasses Mira was making fun of.

Soon many of us head inside to work in the kitchen. It's crowded around the central island. Our new recruits are cutting pumpkin cookies with Mira. Frida's baking pumpkin pie with me. I grimace because Mira just told me a couple hours ago how stupid these Halloween traditions are. But, true to character, Mira isn't just baking, she's telling us ghost stories and sharing recipes with spices and herbs. She even suggests adding an aphrodisiac, but Maddie puts a stop to that. Really, Mira's the most witchy of us all.

Mira starts telling all of us about this Lady Gwynn character while sprinkling an orange pumpkin cookie. Gwynn is some headless ghost in a white dress with a black pig. But I cringe thinking about any black animal right now. A black pig reminds me of my nightmare of riding the black horse. And that makes me remember the visitor last night.

"Mira," I interrupt, "did Alondra ever tell you anything about a haunting in the forest in Alabama?"

She grows a sly smile. "Are you planning a conjuring with the students tonight, Katie? That's the other reason I couldn't resist coming."

"What's she planning, Meer?" asks Courtney excitedly.

Josie stops putting candy eyes on pigs in blankets, so they look like mummies, and Frida turns from the stove beside me.

"In my Book of Shadows, *Broomstick*, Alondra said she used to exorcise ghosts," I explain. "One that she kept mentioning was this poltergeist that haunted Winona in Alabama. Well, the girl, now a woman, came to us last night during our Sabbath. Winona was so desperate, she said that her ghost had returned, apparently to the same house that she lived in as a little girl. She said the ghosts appear for a haunting at the start of every year. So tomorrow, she's asked that I go to her house in Alabama and try to get rid of this spirit. She said the spirit is now haunting her little girl, Kathy."

Mira's eyes are wide at this point. I'm not sure if she's about to make another snide remark or if she's genuinely surprised.

"How deliciously blasphemous, Cadence," Mira finally says, laughing. "You've been asked to honor a demon from hell on All Saints' Day."

"What? No, I've been asked to stop a haunting."

Mira shakes her head and turns serious.

"Winona was a devil," Mira says. "That's what Alondra told me. The girl drove all the head witches in the world nuts after Alondra performed an exorcism on her. Winona was empathic and perfect for, probably, the worst poltergeist haunting in the South. Alondra always felt terrible about the whole thing. She said she felt responsible for the family's problems even up to the time of her passing. It was one of the greatest things she knew she couldn't fix before leaving for the Summerland." Then Mira annoyingly grows silent, almost purposefully making the suspense simmer. She finally says, "Story goes, guys, Winona was possessed by a demon. What was called in ancient Sumeria an Ekimmu. Winona tormented her younger sister, Melanie, slashing her with a knife, constantly pulling out clumps of her hair, and once even throwing her down the stairs. But it gets weirder. That would be normal poltergeist shit. Winona's parents claimed that as the haunting grew stronger, the house's foundation started shaking. Toys and even their beds were seen floating in midair in their bedroom. And once, her mother claimed, Winona scurried on all fours across the room like a spider, climbed up the wall, and hung upside down. That's not a haunting, Windstorm, that's possession stuff.

"Alondra told me it took them all night to exorcise the demon from Winona. She says she had witnessed portals opening in that house that had given her nightmares ever since. This is Alondra we're talking about, Cadence. Yeah, the same Alondra who was known everywhere at the time as a ghost hunter. She knew more about the supernatural than, probably, anyone. She had been obsessed with it ever since she was a little girl. That's what led her to our craft. Anyway, the house in Geneva, Alabama, you're talking about totally freaked *her* out.

"But Alondra succeeded with her exorcism. At first. This house is terrible, guys, because it became stronger through Hecate. Through witches. Alondra told me that the reason the place grew so much power afterward was not only because Winona was empathic and was channeling poltergeists, but because powerful witches were using the house to sabotage Alondra's power. Witches from all over the world had cursed the grounds of that house to stop Alondra from casting in Hawthorne. And they did such a good job that no one, not even Alondra herself, could fix it afterward."

"Then I should go there tomorrow," I say, nodding my head. "I need to help Winona. You even said Alondra wanted to help them."

"You can't help Winona, Cadence," Mira says, laughing harder than ever.

"Why? I had a wandering last night and saw some of that haunting, from the past, with my own eyes. There's something about her house that is threatening our coven, and I need to fix it."

"Alondra said Winona was murdered," Mira says, shaking her head. "That's what made Melanie and her mother finally go berserko. I doubt you saw Winona. Maybe you saw her ghost? Alondra told me she couldn't help the family because there's no family left to help. The place is abandoned."

"No, Mira, I saw Winona too," says Maddie. "I spoke with her. She told me about Kathy. It sounds so terrible for that little girl. She said it's just her and Kathy living in the house now. The ghosts are affecting children again."

"Maybe you saw Melanie claiming to be Winona?" Mira shakes her head. "But if you saw either one, watch your back. Even Alondra feared what they had become."

"No, I spoke with Winona," Maddie says.

"But then she disappeared," says Mandy, folding her arms across the kitchen island pensively. "We never saw her after we returned to the house."

"This is sick, Meer," says Courtney.

"I told you we'd have fun here," Mira quips.

"I think I should check the place out after the party," I say. "If there's anything I can do to help them, I'll do it. We can at least try and take a look at the place."

"Far out," says Courtney, opening her eyes wide.

"Well, count me in, Windstorm," says Mira with a shrug. "I'm always game for a good Samhain haunting."

"After the party tonight, Mira," says a male voice. It's Bryce carrying a bunch of shopping bags. "It's great to see you."

"Hey, Bryce," says Mira with a wave. "I was telling Cadence that all this preparation is for nothing. I think the only guests you're gonna get are in this room."

Bryce shakes his head and winks at me. Then he puts a finger to his lips. "Don't tell anyone. Some honoree of the Psi Kappa Psi fraternity invited his whole chapter." Then he drops all the bags on the counter, walks over to me, and gives me a hug. "Cadence's party's gonna be amazing."

4

MY PARTY

"Told you," Bryce says, raising a red plastic cup in a toast.

He's standing beside me by the stairs. Of course he was right. Bryce is always right. We decorated and transformed Alondra's quaint Southern antebellum mansion into a haunted house—with plastic webs, orange streamers, and candlelight. We laid pumpkins and skulls everywhere with small purple lights along the carpet. And students came to my party. Sort of. I mean it's hard to tell, with all their costumes, who anyone is. Some might not be from Hawthorne University.

Frida greets a mummy and a lady in a white dress and crown, I think it's supposed to be a prom queen, at the front door.

"You did it," Bryce says again, toasting to me.

"But if more kids show up, we might be breaking a city ordinance."

"You don't know what a fraternity is like without a frat house," he says, shaking his head. "This works great for them, babe."

"Yeah? What happens when underaged students start joining you for a drink?" I ask, tapping his red cup with a black fingernail, raising an eyebrow.

"You want me to card them by the door?" Then he hands me a red cup he was hiding in his other hand. "Jeez, Katie, you're being a downer, like Mandy. I tell you this was a great idea."

"I hoped this would bring back some of the tradition from the Billington House," I say with a nod. "Bring back some of Alondra's old magic."

"It will." He sips his cup again and then turns serious. "Seriously, I think this was a really good idea."

"Hey Ms. Wallace!" cries a girl in a checkered skirt, red shirt, and large black witch hat. She's a sorority snoot and I honestly think these are her regular clothes, sans the witch hat. In the olden days, I wouldn't even wave to a sorority sister. But times have changed now that I've graduated and I'm a teaching assistant, I suppose.

"Hi, Doctor Wallace," she says to Bryce. "Hey, what are you two supposed to be? What's with your black robe and dark makeup? Cool."

"They're Druid cloaks, Samantha," Bryce answers.

"Hmm...like...*witches*?" the girl asks with too smug a smile.

I'll share a little secret. Being a witch in Hawthorne is not that much of a secret anymore. Everyone acts like they don't know what we do, but they do. Just, unlike you, they don't know that my magic is real.

"Well, you two look awesome," she says. "Thanks so much for inviting my chapter, professor. Guess what I am?" She runs her finger along the brim of her huge black hat.

"Most of the party is out back," I say with a chuckle. "Or you can hang out in the adjoining room by the patio. We're leaving the sliding door open."

"I know. That's what the other witch over there told me." And she cocks her head back, gesturing to Frida.

"Bro!" cries a guy across the entryway. He's wrapped in bandages. Another mummy. "Bro!"

"Gotta go, Cadence," Bryce says. "More guests have arrived."

But before Bryce can run off, I grab his elbow. "Seriously, Bryce, watch the crowds. And the drinks. We're gonna get into a lot of trouble with the school."

"Don't worry, babe. I already got the okay from the dean."

"What about cops?"

"R-e-l-a-x babe." And he smiles and gently pecks me on the cheek. Then he whispers in my ear, "You've done great."

He throws an arm around the mummy by the door, and they head down our purple-lit hallway.

Then, of all weird things, I hear the voices of children squeaking under the noise. "Trick or treat." Frida smiles wide and kneels at the door before three kids in costumes, loving it. One tyke is dressed as Mario from Mario Brothers, another is some princess in a dress, and a third is an astronaut. We're not getting a whole lot of children. I think my friends did too good a job of making the front yard super spooky.

"Trick or treat," they squeak again.

"Hey, kids," Frida says. "But we don't have any candy."

Wait, I have candy. Shit, I've been planning this party for months. I run over to a small table by the door and grab some Hershey's. I rush over to the door. Luckily, I don't have my hood over my head, but I've got plenty of black makeup. The kids don't seem to mind. They think it's a costume, like the sorority witch.

"Thank you."

Before I can leave the doorway, my fat gray cat, Whiskers, leaps into my arms from outside. I think he's freaked out by the crowds. I run my hand along his soft gray fur.

"Shh, it's okay," I say, kissing my cat's head.

"Frida, you got this? There's more candy stashed under the table."

"But I don't think any more kids will have the nerve to come up to the house, Katie," Frida says with a laugh. "Have fun. I'll close the front door and join you guys in the back after nine."

"Thanks, Frida."

And I'm off to try to have a little fun myself.

Aside from the purple lights, it's dark in my main hallway. I pass the dining room, holding and petting my cat. It's become our party storage room. I see a girl in a black cloak, her black hair in a ponytail, rummaging through bags. That's Josie.

The techno music gets louder and louder as I approach my living room. The living room, normally chic with a white leather sofa and thick white carpet, is full of candles and violet lighting. And it's misty from our fog machine. People in costumes are just swaying and bumping into each other. But the music is coming from outside. Shoving past shoulders and bodies, I make it to the open sliding glass door.

Outside is far worse. Beyond a ton of costumed bodies holding contraband drinks, Natasha and Mandy are trying to corral people in line by the wooden stage for our costume contest. I laugh.

I put my cat down on the patio by the glass door, and he scurries off into the backyard. Then I pick a very nice unoccupied column to lean on.

And then...nothing. That feels nice. After all the party planning, I can just do nothing but lean against a column and watch. I love that. I don't feel like dancing or socializing—I just want to enjoy the outdoors.

Our main central bonfire isn't lit; it's been replaced by small ones that light up the whole yard. Firelight flickers along the shadowed surrounding trees. Diana is a full moon and huge above me amongst the stars. Beautiful. The moon would be brighter if it weren't for all the fire, candles, and occasional flashing lights, I suppose. I was afraid it would rain, but Mira assuaged my fears over the weather and, as usual, she was right.

I feel peace. There are no hell-raising rides on black Pukas or visions of owls or archenemy ravens. No headless ladies in white dresses with black pigs strolling in. No ghosts creeping about the woods. It's just me standing on my patio, arms folded over my black cloak, being entertained by the crowds of students in costumes dancing in my backyard. I spot clowns, ghosts, devils, angels, vampires, and zombies all swaying to the music. By the stage a disk jockey, a friend of Bryce's wearing a 70s disco outfit, is playing music through two huge speakers. At the other side of my yard, I catch Josie and Jessica helping my brother, Damie, fill a large silver tub of water with apples.

I sip my drink. It's sweet mead. I chuckle. Only Bryce would hand me that. You know, I first met Bryce when he was making this stuff, a few years back, at Beltane.

Mandy is so wrong about Halloween. This is what Halloween is all about. Just everyone pretending to be different from their normal selves, acting spooky or funny, yapping and laughing together, and just having plain fun. I laugh as a boy in a clown outfit struggles to move his flubby costume around the tub to reach that apple stem.

"Katie. Katie." That's Frida. She's rushing around bodies near the sliding door. Maddie's right beside her.

"What is it? What's the matter, guys?"

"Party crasher," Maddie says.

"What do you mean?" Then my eyes open wide as I remember the last time Frida ran to me like this. "*Enora!?*"

Frida shakes her head and actually laughs. "Worse."

"*Worse than Enora!?*"

"The dean, Katie," says Frida with a nod, laughing. "Kenosha says she needs to speak with you alone. She looks really angry."

"Yeah, probably because of all this, guys!" I exclaim, pointing to the hundred bodies in my yard. I turn from my friends to the crowd of students to my left, then back to Frida again. And then I look down at my cup of mead. "Shit." Well, so much for peace.

"I don't know," Frida says. "She said she'll meet you upstairs. Upstairs is the only quiet area in the house, I think."

"Okay, Frida. Did you lock the front door?"

"They'll just go around to the back," Maddie says with a shrug.

"What about trick or treaters?"

"There really weren't any anymore," Frida replies. "It's late."

"Okay, you two have fun. I'll go talk with her."

5

THE DEAN

MY BEDROOM LOOKS QUIET, BUT THE KIDS PARTYING IN THE BACKYARD, visible through the floor-to-ceiling window, *look* deafening. I don't think I've ever seen so many people standing in my backyard. Like Frida said, upstairs is the quietest place in the house. The lights are off. I get it, if Kenosha had turned them on, the huge window behind her would have acted as a beacon, and every eye outside would have turned to look at us in this room. Kenosha would hardly be able to have a private talk with me.

Kenosha is sitting in a leather chair in front of the window. It's Kenosha, all right, the dean of Hawthorne University. But she's not wearing professor clothes. She's taken her wig off and has on her forest green witch cloak—it looks older than our black ones.

I close the bedroom door behind me.

"Sit down, Windstorm," Kenosha says, gesturing toward the bed. That makes me mad. Come on, this is *my* bedroom.

"Go on, sit," she infernally requests again. "You have a lot of guests to attend to. I won't be long. I just want a quick word."

I hesitantly sit down on *my* mattress facing her. Damn, if we're not supposed to be holding a party, I'm in trouble. Between scattered bonfires is a field of bodies. In the center a line of costumed revelers are holding their red plastic cups—*contraband* cups full of beer if they are freshman. And all these costumed guys and gals are in line before our makeshift stage. Or they're gathering by a crowd to my right bobbing for apples.

Onstage is a lady in a long, flowing renaissance outfit and a tall white headdress. She's supposed to be Marie Antoinette, I think. It's an impressive costume because the wig and dress are huge. Marie Antoinette is standing and showing off to all the revelers and, even from here, I can hear clapping. Maddie told me that we'd gauge winners by the level of applause—not the most accurate way to yield votes, but that's Maddie.

"Enjoying the party?" I quip.

"I think it was a mistake for a professor to organize this," Kenosha says, glancing over her shoulder. "It's unprofessional of Bryce. For you, as a graduate student, it's not so terrible. But I'm most disappointed with your husband. But—" She irritatingly sighs. "I suppose Alondra enjoyed a party or two when she was younger. Still, she never celebrated Halloween with outsiders of our pentacle. She knew how to keep her professional life separate from her social life."

"She ran an *honors* program with mandrake," I blurt.

Shut up, Cadence!

But, boy, I can't help it. I really just hate Kenosha these days. And I'm not good at hiding my emotions. I've been fighting with her a lot lately. Why? She's slave-driving my husband. He just started as a professor this year, but he works like crazy day and night under her tutelage. She's also bossy as hell toward me, his TA, and over my business with *my* coven.

"You and Bryce need boundaries," she lectures on. "You aren't students anymore. And, as I said, Alondra never dressed up in costumes."

"Then you never knew her."

Okay, that really pisses her off. She stiffens and straightens her green cloak. But before she offers her rebuttal, there's a scream. It makes us both jump. It sounds like it's coming from downstairs. I hear someone run up a few steps to the hallway.

"It's just some guy trying to scare people downstairs, guys," Maddie says. Of course, Maddie's quick response tells me she's obviously standing beside the bedroom eavesdropping.

"If you object to Bryce holding the party," I say to Kenosha, heaving a sigh, "maybe you should talk to him, not me."

"Forget it, Cadence. I didn't come here to talk about Halloween parties. I'm not here as the dean of Hawthorne. I'm here as a fellow witch. I need to speak with you about your wandering last night. Bryce said you saw a vision of the house in Geneva Forest. He even said Winona came to the house yesterday asking you to go there. I came here to warn you. Alondra and I spent years trying to repair the damage we did to that house. In fact, it was that haunting that caused us to drift apart. I suggest —not as your dean, but as a fellow high priestess, and your friend—that you stay away. There's powerful dark left-sided magic there."

It grows quiet. Well, not really. There's still shouting and music bouncing off the walls, but the two of us stop yapping for a moment.

I gaze at the party through the window again. Now atop the stage is a man in an eighteenth-century vampire outfit. It's another really great costume, very "Draculaesque." People really go all out in Hawthorne on Halloween, you know.

When I turn back to Kenosha, I gasp. A black-hooded figure has taken the place of the green one in the shadows. Behind her hooded cloak I can barely recognize a pale face. But I'd recognize those green eyes anywhere. It's Alondra.

Willow can't be trusted.

Then, as quickly as my former teacher appeared, she's gone, and Kenosha's back in her place staring at me. She's quickly looking all about the room.

"What was that?" Kenosha asks. "What did you just see, Cadence?"

Go tomorrow.

"What are you seeing?" Kenosha's head is snapping around, looking all around the room. "Or hearing? Tell me. What is it? I feel a presence in this room right now. What is it?" Kenosha stands up. "You have to tell me, Cadence. Seeing Winona was not a good sign. That house is evil. Alondra and I, along with many other witches, spent years trying to shield our covens from it. Any vision you see or hear, you have to tell me about."

"I don't have to tell you a thing."

"Alondra didn't invite me to the school only as a dean, Cadence. I didn't come only to teach in the university."

I see a zombie walking onstage now. He's doing this stupid zombie dance, and the crowd's loving it. His performance is better than the costume. Maddie didn't figure that part out, did she? He might win applause just by moving around like a fool. I'm afraid that when I look back I will see Alondra's ghost again. I turn back and, thankfully, it's still Kenosha.

"Tell me," she insists. "What or who did you see?"

"Alondra."

"Yes," Kenosha says, searching the room again. "Yes, you told me you've been seeing her on campus." She shakes her head. "But I don't think that was Alondra. Alondra's gone to the Summerland. What did this spirit tell you?"

"To go to the house tomorrow."

"Oh, Cadence," Kenosha says, heaving a sigh, "you can't, I tell you. You'll be away from your hallowed ground. Your magic will be weak. You don't know enough of the arts to face it."

"I can bring Mira."

"Even her knowledge can't help."

"Then I can bring you."

She nods for a moment. But then she shakes her head. "I know better than to ever go there again."

"I need to go. I feel like Alondra wants me there to make things right. And Winona was telling us about her poor daughter."

Kenosha shakes her head again. But she grows silent. She seems afraid. There's something about this house in Alabama that's really freaking her out. And anything that scares this powerful witch is unsettling to me.

"I saw you last night when I was in a trance," I say. "You and Alondra were fighting. You were in the house, pinned to a wall, upside down. You weren't contending with ghosts, you were fighting with Alondra. She was casting a spell on you, wasn't she?"

"I told you the two of us fought in that house."

"Winona seemed desperate. If there's anything I can do for her daughter, I'll do it. You've said many times that my power can be used for good. I need to see if I can help her. I'm the Hawthorne Witch now."

"Bryce said you rode a Puka last night?" Kenosha says. "A Puka is a trickster during Halloween. Alondra's not telling you to go, Cadence. This is a Samhain trick. It's a Puka."

"Tell me what you were fighting about, then maybe I'll avoid the house. Alondra's asking me to go for some reason."

But, of course, as is customary with these old witches, just like my former teacher-witch, Alondra, Kenosha clams up. They're always doing that. They're so irritatingly secretive.

"Just tell me what you were fighting about. If I know more, I can make a decision."

Kenosha runs a hand over her bald head. She nods.

"I don't like talking about this. I'm not proud of it. The witch counsel decided to take Alondra's book. What should have been my coven's book. *Broomstick. Broomstick* is how we met. She met me in New Orleans searching for my Crescent coven after she found the book. But I had heard of Alondra even before I met her. At the time, your teacher was known everywhere around the occult world as a powerful supernatural spirit hunter. Believe it or not, she offered me your book when we met because it was Escoba's. Escoba, as you know, was the founder of my Crescent coven."

"I don't see how it could be only Escoba's," I object. "I've seen Akkadian symbols from Mesopotamia. And spells from Celtic sources. Some of the ancient writing isn't in Alondra's handwriting. Some ancient spells look far older than Escoba."

"Just because Escoba practiced hoodoo doesn't mean she didn't study ancient rites."

"Is that why you fought Alondra? You wanted our book?"

"Of course I wanted *Broomstick*. But out of kindness, and because of her personal discovery of the book, I didn't take it. My sisters were furious. The book's very presence is said to hold enough power to act as a talisman that can protect against ghosts. Its mere presence can shield a witch from the psychological forces of Ekimmu and Alu. Probably, I suspect, because it was used by Escoba to fight poltergeists in hoodoo rituals hundreds of years ago. Yes, it's possible the book is older than Escoba herself. But that's not why we fought. Winona's family, just like they came to you last night, came to me in New Orleans for help. You have to understand, Cadence, that these hauntings have to first be investigated. There are a lot of people who think their house is haunted when, in fact, it's a figment of their imagination, madness, or a prank. Well,

Winona was very real. The ground was ripe for spiritual energies, and Winona, just like you and your teacher, had a gift. Winona was empathic. When I realized her haunting was very real, I realized I needed to get help."

"Alondra?"

"Yes. Alondra. But back then, I went to hauntings to help people. Your teacher, Alondra, had far different motivations. She used hauntings to understand the supernatural. Her curiosity, you see, is what ruined her life. Her devotion to learning everything, every piece of knowledge, left or right, led to her misery, Cadence. And that's what caused our fight. When Alondra started experimenting with black magic, we had our falling out.

"Although I knew I needed her aid, and the help of her book, I was already distancing myself from her due to her experimentation. And it was not only her evil left-sided magic, but her ego, something voodoo is strongly against, that came to the forefront. Her selfish desire was making her dangerous. She was ignoring the council, just as she was ignoring me. Everything was about her and no one could reach her. She was young, younger than you. You don't know the young, reckless Alondra like I did. Age, you know, has its way of calming one's spirit. Back then, Alondra was completely out of control."

"I remember her spunk," I say with a laugh. My teacher's arrogance was one of the things that was so infuriating about her. But that was Alondra and I loved her.

"Yes, but when she was younger, she was disrespectful. Reckless. So... the council of witches, practitioners of magic from West Africa to England, decided to take her Book of Shadows and Grimoire. We decided to take *Broomstick*. Of course, as you can imagine, taking it didn't come without a fight."

Then Kenosha falls silent again. The room is quiet. And it seems the house is quieter too.

"I cast a spell on her, Cadence," Kenosha says. "Yes, I did. I'm not proud of it. It's shameful and one of the worst things I ever did to anyone. I didn't want to do it. I loved Alondra. We were very good friends. But no one could persuade her to follow the right path. Not even the man she fell in love with. She was becoming the most powerful witch in America, perhaps the world, but she was becoming evil. You know that better than anyone. You yourself tried to put a stop to it.

"But we all make mistakes. Winona's house was mine. In order to stop Alondra, I cursed it. I thought that a little evil for the sake of a little good was the right thing to do. It never is. My magic and Winona's empathic power was enough to damn the ground. That's what you saw me fighting. See, I wasn't just fighting Alondra, Cadence, I was fighting the evil in that house. It is not just a haunted ground, it's a cursed one—cursed by both me and your teacher." She puts her head in her hands and stops for a moment. "That's why I don't like talking about it."

"But that must be why Alondra's telling me to go, Kenosha!" I say. "If ghosts are haunting the house again and threatening Winona's daughter, I have to try to help the family. This could be what Alondra needs to finally be freed to the Summerland. Mira told me this was the one wrong she couldn't right before she died."

"Cadence, I helped Alondra protect that house," she says, nodding. "Yes, I did. For years afterward, the two of us cast *shield* spells after Mabon every year. To protect people *outside* the property. That land is completely cursed."

"I don't think Alondra made it to the Summerland when she passed, Kenosha," I say, shaking my head. "I hate to say it, but I think she's trapped. That's why I keep seeing her. And now her spirit is trying to get me to go to the house to help finally set her free."

"Cadence," Kenosha says, shaking her head, "Alondra believed she had the right to learn left-sided magic to combat left-sided forces. Abaddon witches. I didn't even believe there was such a thing as pure evil. So when Alondra studied it, I viewed her as creating it. So I fought *her*. I didn't believe there was any other evil to fight. But after Winona's curse, I tell you I was wrong. Evil is all you will find from that place. Evil, Cadence."

"Come with me tomorrow then. I just have to go there to see for myself. You're powerful, Kenosha. If it's too dangerous, you can help me. And I can see if I can help Alondra there."

"Even if you're right about Alondra, and her spirit is summoning you to go," she says quietly, shaking her head, "it's too dangerous."

Then Kenosha leans forward and searches my eyes. "You're not still going to go?" she says. "After everything I just said? You know I didn't want to tell you that story, Cadence. I'm not proud of it. I made my mistakes, just like Alondra did. We've paid for them. Now that cursed house is the manifestation of them. Stay away from there, I tell you."

"But Alondra's spirit is asking me to go."

Kenosha squints her eyes and stares. Then she shakes her head violently and jumps up. "No, I forbid this," she snaps. "You will not go. I am also your dean. Do not leave Hawthorne tomorrow. I cannot allow you—"

"Blessed be, Willow," I say, finally standing up too. "You can't forbid me to do anything. You can fail me, expel me—you are the dean of Hawthorne University, you can do whatever you want to my education—but I am still the high priestess and leader of my coven. I am the Hawthorne Witch."

"Why are you not listening to—"

"You're not listening to me! Alondra's asked me to go, I tell you."

"She isn't! That's not her!"

I turn my back on her, open my bedroom door, and make my way back to the stairs. It's mean, but she's upsetting me again. She's got such nerve. Maddie, of course, is midway down the steps, eavesdropping.

"You really saw Alondra, Katie?" Maddie says in a hushed whisper.

Kenosha rushes by us, nearly knocking me over on the stairs. "You must be the most stubborn witch in the world, *Hawthorne Witch*," Kenosha says. "You may even be as arrogant as the last one." Then she rushes to the front door, dodging a clown and a guy in a large hot dog outfit. All the people in the room stare at her—because she's the dean. Then she throws open the door and leaves in a huff.

"Boy, she's angry. Well, at least she's not mad about the party." Maddie chuckles nervously. "We are still going tomorrow, babe?"

I heave a long sigh and look back upstairs. For a moment, I recall Alondra in her last months, studying in her study upstairs or sleeping in her bed. Her bedroom is my bedroom now. And back then, too, I had infernal meetings with a powerful witch—Alondra, and she was sometimes just as infuriating as Kenosha. Alondra and I never got along great either. But, boy, what I'd do to talk about all this with my teacher now.

"Let's just get back to the party, Maddie."

"The party's kinda dead."

"What do you mean?"

"Well, afraid Mira was right," Maddie says with a shrug. She leans on the staircase railing. "While you had your talk, a lot of students escaped through the side yard. People are meeting somewhere else for their festivities later tonight. They came to show up, but they're off on their own now. Not many drinkers at Dr. Wallace's house."

She's right. I notice the house is much quieter. But maybe everyone ran away after seeing the dean?

I sigh again. "Okay, Maddie."

"It's okay, babe." Maddie smiles and rubs my back. "All of us are still here. And Bryce managed to keep some of his friends around. And Gilda just got here and wants to see you. We're all here, just like we'll all be with you tomorrow."

"You think we should go, Maddie? Did you hear her warning? She seems spooked by that place."

"Think of the poor little girl, Kathy, Cadence. Yeah, I think the Hawthorne Witch should at least try to help. If it's too weird, we can just turn around and drive home."

6

———

THE SAMHAIN WITCH

IT'S FOGGY AND DARK—NOT TOO UNEXPECTED, I SUPPOSE, RIGHT? WE'RE going to a haunted house, after all. I fell asleep leaning against the passenger door of Bryce's BMW. Now I'm stretching my arms, watching drops of rain trickle down the window. Tall, dark, and handsome is driving us past tons of trees, telling me that we've entered another forest and are almost there. The trees here remind me of Hawthorne, but with today's mist...it's creepier.

My brother, Damie, and my best friend, Maddie, are sitting behind us. And Mira and Courtney are behind us in a black van. I couldn't get anyone else to go. I don't think it was the haunted stuff; it was just too short notice after Halloween. Bryce and I have a lecture tomorrow too. And that means I have to prepare notes for our students tonight—if we survive whatever it is we're facing here.

"You still awake, babe?" asks Bryce as he turns the car onto an even more desolate road, heading uphill.

"Um-hmm." I stretch again. "Just thinking."

"About what?"

"Oh, I don't know, Bryce. How about how Kenosha thinks we're all going to die tonight?"

"I'd be dying with you."

"You're not scared, Bryce?" Maddie asks with a chuckle.

"I am scared. But I don't think Kenosha's right. I don't believe ghosts harm people. Alondra taught us that ghosts are more like an energy, like a force. The only thing they can do is get into one's mind. Anyway, I'm sitting beside the famous Hawthorne Witch. And she brought her book."

Yep, my ancient book *Broomstick*, Escoba's Book of Shadows and Grimoire, is sitting on my lap. And why not? Kenosha said it acts like some kind of special talisman against ghosts.

"But Bryce," says Maddie, "according to Mira, Winona was possessed by ghosts and demons. Madness threw her sister down the stairs. I'd say that was physical harm."

"Thanks a lot, Maddie," Bryce says.

"Cadence said Alondra's spirit told her to come," Damie says. "If anything, we're being led by a ghost to come here."

Which is super creepy too, isn't it?

I heave a sigh again. Of course Maddie's right. So is Damie.

I shake my head hard, fold my arms, and say, "I don't know, guys, all I know is that, for some reason, we have to be here. Alondra beckoned me. I know Kenosha said it could be a trap, but I *felt* Alondra tell me to come. Just like I've been feeling her all around campus. There are no Halloween tricks. I know she spoke with me. She wants us here."

But I stop yapping. Because right in front of me on the road is something creepier than ever.

Now I don't watch many horror movies—I sort of live one—but right in front of Bryce's car is this rickety old wooden bridge covered in white mist. Not only is it making my mind run wild, thinking a swamp creature is going to climb over the edge and attack us, the bridge looks ready to collapse under the weight of Bryce's car.

Bryce inches his BMW along very slowly, and I can hear the wooden boards creaking.

"Maybe this is what Kenosha meant when she said something was going to harm us?" Damien says.

"Shut up, Damie!" Maddie says, hitting his arm. "God, will you?"

"Sorry," he says with a chuckle.

"We're through." Bryce sighs. Then he looks at the rearview mirror. "Not so sure about Mira though."

And Bryce stares at his rearview mirror as we wait for Mira to make the same death-defying drive over the condemned bridge with her clunky black minivan.

We drive on while I start thumbing through Bryce's navigation on his dashboard. We're almost there, according to the map.

Looking through the window between tall, thick trees and fog, there's little visibility. And the road's getting very bumpy. We've left asphalt and are driving on a dirt road—or a muddy one. The road is broken up with pieces of asphalt between rocks and mud.

"We should have left earlier," I say. "The sun is nearly down."

"Haunted houses are better at night, sis," quips my brother.

"Will you just shut up, Damien!" Maddie says, hitting his arm again.

"Sorry, Madds."

"Katie, is there any sense of why Alondra wants us here?" asks Maddie.

"Something to do with the past. Kenosha had a huge falling out with Alondra over my book because of this house. I think she wants to fix the harm done to it."

I run my fingers along the worn leather cover of my ancient book. I'm so glad I brought it.

"Well, here it is," Bryce says, pointing.

I look up and gasp. This is far, far worse than the bridge. Before me is a lone broken structure enveloped in white mist. A house? No, not really. It's swallowed up by trees. The first-level windows are broken, and I see branches growing inside. Most of the roof's tiles are missing. The driveway is eaten by bushes and wild grass. And saplings are growing in the most awkward places. A tree's sprouting up beside the front door. The front door is boarded up, and there are red spray-painted lines on the wooden boards. Mira's van is idling behind us.

"What the fuck is that?" asks Maddie.

"A haunted house," I say.

"I don't like this, guys," Maddie says. "Let's go. I wanted to help a family, Cadence. Winona's not living there. Neither is any little girl. No family's there."

"Alondra wanted you to come *here*?" Bryce asks me. He's not being mean—he just doesn't get it either.

"It's the right address," Damie says. "Look, we didn't spend four hours on the highway for nothing." Then my brother throws open the door and hops out. You gotta admit, he's got guts.

It's so misty outside that it feels like it's raining. White wisps surround us. And I feel the moisture against my cheeks. It smells nice. Like Hawthorne, with a pine and fresh air smell. I like that forest smell.

"Let me get our cloaks." Bryce walks back to his trunk. "If we're going to go in there, we might as well look the part."

"Who says we have to go in, Bryce?" I ask. "I came here to help a little girl. Maddie's right, no girl's living inside there."

"Got that right," Maddie says.

"Come on, Kate," insists Damien with a grin. "Let's just have a quick look."

"*Hey, guys!*"

Mira shouts the words behind me. She's such a bitch, she did it just to freak us out. She and Courtney are already wearing their black robes and dark makeup. I muse that if anyone drove up and saw our get-ups and makeup with this backdrop they'd flip a U-turn and race off.

"This is so cool," Mira says, staring at the house. "We should be doing haunts more often, Cadence."

"Far out, Meer," Courtney says, nodding with a gaping grin. "You know what this means? You guys really did see a ghost last Sabbath, didn't you? What freak girl would ask you to come *here* and help get rid of spirits? Where? It's like the house was swallowed up by the woods."

"Yeah, so are we going in?" asks Mira with too big a grin.

"I think we should just leave," I say, glancing at Maddie. Unlike my brother, she looks totally freaked out. "There's no family to help, Mira."

But my book falls out of my hands. It spins on the ground, round and round, reminding me of a compass needle. We're all staring at it. Then it rises a little on its side and...launches like a projectile toward the house, crashing through glass.

Then we're just staring at the broken window.

What... the... fuck...

"*Broomstick* wants you to go in," Damie says.

"No choice now," Mira agrees with a laugh, sounding way too excited. "Unless you want to go home without your book."

Bryce hands me my black cloak. He nods too.

I begrudgingly don my cloak. I must admit it gives me a little confidence. Then we make our way slowly to the boarded-up door.

There's no doorknob. I try pushing the boards and it just creaks open. Then a piece of wood nearly lands on my foot.

Inside it's pitch black. It's nearly twilight outside, and I can't see the sun in the fog; inside it's like a cave. I think all the overgrowth is covering the windows—or the holes where they once were.

Bryce turns on a very bright flashlight from his car. He shines it along the floor and walls. The walls are caked in mud. His beam lands on my book, now lying further inside the house. I turn on my cellphone light too. There's no carpet on the floor. Or, if there is carpet, it's caked in mud now. Bushes are growing against the walls. Brown grass or moss is growing *inside* the house. It smells musty. That nice fresh woods aroma outside smells spoiled here.

I flash my phone light further down. That's when a shadow rushes by the wall. I shriek. It looked like a human figure.

I run right back outside.

"What's the matter!" cries Maddie.

"Fuck!" I cry. "What the fuck! I mean...shit! What the fuck was that?"

"What's wrong, babe?" asks Bryce.

We're all outside again. I'm breathing heavily. Everyone is staring at me. Didn't they see the shadow?

"There's someone in there," I say to all of them.

"Cadence, I think maybe—" But Maddie can't finish her sentence. There's a thud. It sounds like something really heavy fell upstairs.

"You didn't see it?" I ask everyone. They all shake their heads.

"Shit," I say. "I mean fucking shit... Guys... I have to get my book."

"Well, we either go back in or we don't," Bryce says. "If you don't want to go in, I can run in and grab it. Either way, we can't just stand here."

"I know," I say.

"You're The Hawthorne Witch, Cadence," Mira reminds me with an infernal grimace. "Maybe whoever's in there should be scared of you."

"I opt for staying outside," Maddie says.

Bryce turns to me. He furrows his brow, searching my eyes. "Did you feel anything inside? Beyond what you saw, does it feel safe?"

"How should I know?"

"I was hoping you felt it with your magic," Bryce replies. "Not just saw something."

"I don't feel any magic here. We're far from Hawthorne. Kenosha was right. I don't feel much magic at all. Not from me, anyway."

Damie walks back inside. You must admit, my brother's brave. Or stupid. Before I know it, we're all inside again watching Damie bravely snatch my book from the middle of the house. But even he grabs it quickly and then rushes back to me.

Then the front door slams shut behind us.

"Shit!"

We're closed inside and only our cellphones or Bryce's large flashlight are lighting our way.

"This is ridiculous, Windstorm," Mira says, sounding mad. "Not only are we witches, but you're a high priestess. Why are we afraid?"

"Magic or not, this place—"

We hear howling. It sounds too weird to be the wind.

Of course Mira's right. I mean, really? A slamming door? A foggy bridge on a desolate road? A moving shadow? This is routine haunting stuff. And I am the head witch of my coven.

"Here's your book, sis," Damie says, practically in a whisper. I clutch it tightly under my arm.

We all turn to the sudden sound of running water in an adjoining hallway. That's weird. It sounds like a faucet was turned on. Bryce shines his bright flashlight along the wall. Halfway down the dark hall, water seems to be running from the roof into a puddle on the floor.

"Wow," says Courtney, walking closer.

"What?" asks Mira. "It's just water from the roof."

"Look closer, Meer," Courtney says. "It's running backwards from the floor up to the ceiling! That is so dope."

But none of us wants to look for long. Instead, we inch forward through the hallway and pass into a larger room—or what once was two adjoining rooms. There's a remnant of a couch on the far side. It's in the shape of a couch, anyway, but it's really just a mound of mud. Most of the furniture is just mounds of dirt and mud.

"I saw the shadow here, guys," I say quietly, pointing to a wall.

Flashing her cellphone light against the wall, Courtney screams. A body is reflected back at her.

"It's just your reflection, dummy," Mira says, walking up to it. She taps the wall with her fingernail. "This is glass. Like a sliding glass door. Now there's a wall of mud behind it."

"Katie, your book and teacher got you here," Damie says. "We're here. So now what?"

Red. Red smoke forms. And we all stare at it dumbfounded. At first it's dim, but it grows ever brighter. It's emitting light even when Bryce shines his light away from it. The crimson freaks me out. It is the color I saw, in my vision, in my archenemy Enora's underground lair last year. And I smell it—that familiar horrible stench of sulfur mixed with cinnamon and sandalwood. The same odor I smelled on my ride on the black horse. It's like a red *smell*.

"What is that?" asks Damie.

"Enora," says Mira. And she no longer sounds excited. "This is a trap, Cadence. Let's get out of here. Enora is up to her tricks again."

But we're too late. The red smoke on the other side of the room gets thicker until a witch in a scarlet cloak appears amidst the smoke. She has her hood over her head, but we all know who it is.

"Oh, hi, Katie," the bitch-witch says. "Hi, Raven. So nice to see all of you."

Enora lowers her hood and flashes her infernal smug grin. Her bitch-face is decked in the same goth makeup as ours, but full of devilish nastiness. She raises her fingers, looking around in the darkness, the house now filled with her red smoke.

"What d'ya think?" Enora asks. "Hmm? Quaint, isn't it? It might need a little tidying up, but it's not so bad. A bit dirty, but it holds such promising psychic energy. It's probably the most powerful spot in the entire South. I mean, you can just feel the energy. I love it." She laughs. "That's what you get when you torment two little children. Is that why I'm here?"

"Aren't you in jail?" snaps Mira.

"Aren't you dead?" Enora replies. "I distinctly remember slicing your throat?" The bitch cackles. "Hmm. Oh, but I see the scar on your neck. I did cut your throat, didn't I, Raven? Well, it seems we're finally on true neutral ground, witches. Or have you moved here, Windstorm? Is this your new coven's home?"

"Did you send Winona's spirit to us yesterday?" snaps Maddie.

"You guys want to hear a ghost story?" Enora asks.

She brandishes a knife. It flickers in the light emitted by Bryce's flashlight. But the weapon doesn't really scare me. Just seeing the bitch is scary enough.

"Alondra told me about this house," Enora continues. "She probably didn't tell you, Bryce. Nor you, Raven. Or even you, Cadence. Because I was Alondra's favorite. See, story goes that it was Kenosha who brought Alondra's book, *Broomstick*, here. It belonged to her Crescent coven—"

"Kenosha didn't take her book," I say. "Kenosha would have kept it. And you were never Alondra's favorite, you were cast out. Alondra hated you. Just as Kenosha hates you. Which is why Kenosha sent you to prison. So how are you even here, Enora?"

Damien moves really close to Enora, but the evil witch waves her dagger before him. "Watch it, little Katie's brother," Enora snaps. "Even without magic, I can slice your throat too."

"You're outnumbered, Enora," Bryce says. "Drop the knife. You hold only as much magic as we do."

"Shush, Bryce," Enora says. "I don't want to hear that dull voice. It's so tiresome. Anyway, you know better, high wizard. Don't you see that this is a ceremonial knife? Tell me why you summoned me. I have to admit, I'm very curious. The power here is amazing."

"Wait a minute," I say, "you were summoned here too?"

Bryce's beam of light goes out. All our cellphone lights stop working too. Only the red smoke around Enora remains.

"If the knife cuts," Enora says, looking around the red, smoky room, "blood falls upon this cursed ground, providing a wondrous witch power. I wager a witch probably wouldn't need a coven here. You didn't summon me, little Katie? Hmm. So spirits of Samhain did? Even better. I used them to help break me free from my cell. Now I shall use them to empower me. Or perhaps a deal, witches? Perhaps we can create a new Abaddon coven together right here, right now, in Alabama?"

"None of us are joining you ever again, Panthera!" cries Courtney. "Not after what you did to me, Mira, and Maddie."

"I provided you three a home. We were family, until little Katie here meddled. You three deserted *me*."

"You used them to bleed me!" I cry.

"You hold no power here, Enora," Bryce says.

"Is that right, Bryce?" Enora asks. "Then tell me, why is the room red?"

And, in fact, the whole room is full of her crimson smoke now. It's the only thing lighting it.

I feel afraid. When I'm in a trance, my power gives me confidence. Not here. Here I shudder. So I clutch *Broomstick* tightly in my arms. I can't let it fall now because I need all the magic I can get.

Something feels off. Dark. Cold.

"Did you sacrifice here, Enora?" I ask. "Is that why you're growing power?"

"Not yet," Enora says with a laugh. "All witches have power everywhere, Katie. Or are you so ignorant in our arts that you didn't know that?"

"Put down the knife," warns Damie.

"Can you feel it?" Enora says, ignoring him, walking about the room. She recovers her nasty smugness, twirling her dagger. She laughs. "Can't you just feel it, witches? It's evil. I think we should put the room to a test." She cocks her head back. "How much power does this hallowed ground really hold? Anyone want to bleed with me? If I muster the forces within these walls, I could be the most powerful witch in the whole world! Who needs to bleed you, Cadence? I can summon the magic here and bring it back to Atlanta. I am giving you girls one more chance to join me. How 'bout you, Courtney? Madison? Conjure with me or I'll partake in all this power myself."

But no one says a word. Because we all loathe her.

"Suit yourself," Enora says.

She cuts her forearm with the knife. As the blood drips on the ground, there are screams. They sound like children's screams, making this even creepier, and it echoes all around us. Enora raises her bloody knife high in the air.

"Allow Panthera to recite from *Ars Goetia*," Enora says. "Recite with me, students of Hecate, if you dare. I call forth names of those once summoned by the former Hawthorne high priestess. The witch who empowered this lair. *Adramelch! Beleth! Marduk! Paimon! Balam! Belial!* Sweet Lucifer shine thy light before us, worshippers of Diana and Selene. Satanas, come before me in darkness. *Lux tenebris!* I, Panthera, cast this incantation upon you on this powerful sacred ground. As my blood drips, come to me, *venite foras*, enter Kathy's home. Manifest before her cursed children, Winona and Melanie. Come forth, spirits, on this hallowed day. Again, call out their names with me, witches!"

Her magic is working. My friends are frozen. Damie and Courtney start mouthing the names with her: "*Adramelch! Beleth! Marduk! Paimon! Balam! Belial!*"

∾

I see a vision of a black bird striking a mouse. Then the raven is grabbed by some large creature from...

∾

Kathy's *cursed children?* What does Enora mean, *children?* I thought Kathy was Winona's daughter?

"Did you get the door, Mother?" croaks a quiet voice. "It seems our guests have arrived."

Kathy is Winona and Melanie's mother? And in my vision, the black bird struck down was a raven... A black bird like Amica. Amica is Enora's totem. So... could that mean I was seeing Enora struck down?

"Enora, this isn't right," I say. "This is a trap."

Enora gazes at me and stops her recitation for a moment. Her magic is working. Her eyes are turning a ghastly pearly white. She smiles and says, "You *are* scheming, aren't you, Windstorm? Very good, manifest it before me. I dare you. With the power of this house, I can shield myself against any hex you have planned."

"*Adramelch! Beleth! Marduk! Paimon! Balam! Belial! Venite foras, satanus, en tenebris!*"

All lights go out. It's as if a black curtain doused all the red smoke. It's completely pitch black.

I grope for Bryce's hand, but I can't find it. Maddie cries out behind me. Then Bryce and my brother gasp. Mira and Courtney shout out too. Bryce's hand gropes for mine and he squeezes it tightly. But I can't see a thing. Blind, I clutch my book as tightly as I can in my arms.

"Lux alba!" I cry. But no light comes forth.

There's a hissing sound. Like a snake. Another crash is heard from upstairs. Then I hear a rattle. The ground shakes. There's a growl. Then a clang of metal. And that's all followed by screams—like a thousand little children screaming. But then...far worse. I hear an adult screaming. This scares me most of all because it sounds like Enora and she's in pain. Why would Enora be in pain? She just pompously walked around the room casting her stupid devil spell.

"Lux alba!" I cry desperately. It's still pitch dark.

"Prohibe!" yells Enora. *"Prohibe!"* She's in a panic. "Stay away! *Prohibe! Apage diablo! Probibe! Get back! Get... Stay away from me!"*

A blast of frigid air rushes by my face and, with it, giggling. Children's giggling.

"Prohibe!" cries Enora again in darkness. *"Prohibe!"*

"Lux alba! Lux alba!" I say with her, in a panic.

"I can't see, Cadence!" yells Maddie.

"Stay away from me. Get away!"

"She threw me down the stairs, Mother!"

"Stop it, Melanie! Stop it! They're trying to help you!"

"Winona pushed me. She pushed me, Momma. She pushed me down the stairs!"

There's a skirmish in front of me, where Enora was standing, as if two people are wrestling or boxing in the darkness.

"Verbi devini minister?" croaks a stranger's voice. There's a little girl's laughter among the words. *"Vi veri universum vivus vici. Infirma maga. Infirma. Sanguineus Hawthorne."*

"What's happening!" cries Damie.

I hold my book out with all my concentration and intent. *"Lux alba!"*

Bryce's large flashlight turns back on. All the red smoke is gone.

His beam drifts over Enora. Enora is fighting herself—she is wrestling and twisting on the ground, but there's nothing attacking her. Her whole body is being violently thrown back and forth across the carpet, almost as if she's seizing. She's dropped her dagger. The blade shimmers, reflecting Bryce's beam across the room. Finally a force slides Enora all the way across the room, throwing her hard against the wall. Enora struggles as she's dragged up the wall, her arms and legs spread in an X. She's pinned and cannot move. The flashlight beam shakes over her body because Bryce's hand is shaking. This is just like my vision of Kenosha last night, only Enora is the body right side up in the form of an X. It seems Enora can move only her eyes.

Her eyes move to the right.

A huge shadow creeps slowly across the floor. It's a hunched human figure, covered in filth and wearing only dirty rags. It grabs the wall with sharp, twisted fingernails then slowly crawls up the wall like a spider. When it reaches Enora, it looks like a spider ready to consume its prey.

"Abaddon, Abaddon," croaks the creature. "Abaddon, cold on gray, come with me, sister Lucy, play, play, play? Devil worshipper? More Hawthorne Sinners? Welcome to Sheol. Glory be to God! Another demon has come to save us, Mommy!"

And the creature bursts into laughter. It is a woman's laughter and it echoes all around us.

"Stay away from me!" cries Enora, opening her creepy white eyes wide. "Stay away! Cadence, is this your doing? Did you summon her here to devour me! If you didn't, god, help me! Help me conjure and get rid of this!"

But what even is it? The creature snaps its head toward us like a bird. I see thin, stringy hair, but it's largely bald. Maddie lets out a scream when we see what appears to be a group of thin vipers slithering around the stranger's neck, arms, and legs.

"Wicked witch," it says to Enora. "You satanic, evil witch."

"We can exorcise this," Enora says, horrified. Her eyes are still white, but she's oddly powerless. "Cadence, our magic can rid us of this monster —together!"

The creature's deformed and dirty fingernails glide along Enora's shoulder, then over her face. Enora yells again and manages to turn her head, trying to pull her arm and leg away from the wall, but she can't move.

"Someone come to devour you?" asks the creature. "Come to consume *students* of the Hawthorne coven?"

"I'm not a student of the Hawthorne coven!"

"Shh," says the creature, licking the blood from Enora's arm. "You were."

"*Muta, muta, muta!*" cries Enora.

A flock of black birds explodes out of the creature's grasp, tearing Enora's red cloak, and flutters out into the darkness. Enora's gone.

But the creature isn't. It jumps off the wall and lands upright on the ground. Then, perhaps even more disturbingly, she stands erect like a human. Her eyes are as white as Enora's were before. Pieces of cloth cover her waist. Otherwise she is naked but covered with so much dark filth and muck as to have the mud clothe her.

"Where is the High Priestess of Hawthorne?" asks the creature. "Where is the High Priestess of the Crescent coven? I do not wish to see their disciples tonight. Give me their teachers."

"You sent the ghost to us?" Bryce asks.

"Where is the High Priestess of Hawthorne?" she asks, ignoring Bryce. "Where is the High Priestess of the Crescent coven?"

"Mira," I say, carefully turning from her, "what sort of magic—"

I'm thrown across the room and slammed against the wall. I find it hard to breathe. "Cadence!" I hear my friends exclaim.

This monster has its hand around my neck and is strangling me. I realize my feet are above the ground, and I'm gasping for air as its fingernails stab my skin and its fingers crush my throat. Its dark eyes search my face. It has a horrible, rotten stench. And, worst of all, its gray lips are smiling at me.

"Address your friends. And they follow you? So you are their high priestess? Is that not what you told me during your Sabbath the other night?" She touches my book with a free hand and, mercifully, that makes her let go of my neck. I fall to the ground. "And what do you have here? Your grimoire? Or your Book of Shadows?" I'm holding my book under my arm more tightly than ever. Her grin turns to a scowl and her eyes open wide. "This is the book, Mother! This is the cursed thing! This is the one that cursed us all! Alondra's book is here!"

"Winona?" I ask.

"Melanie." But she says her name absent-mindedly. She's staring at *Broomstick*. It's then I realize that my friends' flashlights are no longer shining on us.

I turn and, in the shadows, Bryce is standing and staring at a wall. His flashlight has fallen from his hand and is casting light in my direction, but it's on the floor. Damien is staring at a wall too. Maddie, Courtney, and Mira are groping the walls as if lost. There's not a sound from them either. Some spell is confusing all of my friends.

"Whatever's going on in this house has nothing to do with us, Melanie," I say.

"Then why do you have her book?" she asks, still staring at it. "Where is Alondra Billington? Is this a trick? Why would she give you her book and not wish to appear herself?"

"Alondra's in the Summerland."

"Liar!" Melanie shouts. She grinds her teeth in rage and shakes her head violently. "I saw her! I saw her walking in the hallway of her house during your witch Sabbath two days ago while your coven sat by the bonfire!" Then, even weirder, the beast's gray lips curl into a smile. "Wait...what is this? Do you hear, Kathy? Do you hear? The Crescent coven high priestess arrives? She comes to visit us too? How delightful."

Melanie laughs. Then her head lurches up and sniffs the air. It can't be her own horrible stench she's smelling.

"Will you fly away like cowardly black birds too?"

I'm thrown against the wall again. Then I feel the cuts from her deformed fingernails along my neck. And once more I can't breathe.

"Willow comes with you? The leader of the Crescent coven? Deny me that? What are you all planning? Trying to hurt us? Get rid of us? There will be no getting rid of anything. Not until we make you and your covens suffer. Not until I bring you the pain we endured. She's hiding in the other room, Momma. Do you see her shaking before us?"

"Yes, dear," says a distant voice. "I see her."

"Bring her out in the open so that I may provide a special greeting. It's been too long."

I'm choking again. Melanie's choking me and I can't speak.

7

____

JUMBEE

My eyes open and my face is warmed by a large central bonfire. I recognize my backyard. A woman in a white dress and white cloth head-dress is crouched down next to me with her arms and head tucked to her chest, looking like a huge alabaster stone. This is a witch's conjuring pose, one I've seen my teacher and enemy Enora assume, but witches wear black. This witch is dark-skinned, wearing all white.

Jumbee, jumbee. Duppy jumbee. Hawthorne turn jumbee.

But I look over my shoulder, and I'm surprised to not see my house. That makes me afraid, for I recognize my trees and grass. This is my backyard, but my house, Alondra's old mansion, is missing.

I feel disoriented. Is this the Summerland? Was I suffocated to death by that monster?

Jumbee, jumbee. Duppy jumbee.

I walk around the white meditative figure. I see a large yellow snake slither over her neck, but somehow this serpent doesn't frighten me.

"Duppy jumbee," says the alabaster orb. *"No. Oh, you don't like jumbees, Cadence? We don't like jumbees either."*

Another dark-skinned lady in a similar white dress appears near the fire. She's twirling round and round. Then comes another. And another. A whole group of these witches with white dresses and headdresses dance around the flames. And many of them carry snakes around their necks too. Then one dancer stops, falls to the ground, and starts shaking as if convulsing.

"Is she all right?" I ask.

The witch, still crouched in a ball under me, laughs. *"Duppy Jumbee, jumbee, jumbee."*

She finally lifts her head and I recognize her face. I've seen her ghost spirit before and, for the first time, I lose all fear. I feel tranquil. This is Escoba, my ancestor. But she can't be here. She lived two hundred years ago. And she's not transparent like the ghost figure I've seen in the past. This time it's as if she is really right in front of me.

"Cher Mambo Cadence," Escoba says. She rises and wraps her arms around me, hugging me tight. Then she kisses my cheek. "Mambo Escoba needs the book to help you. Where's my book? I can help you, child, if you bring the book."

The dancers in white are shaking around us, and some have fallen over the grass as if seizing.

"Jumbee, jumbee," says a dancer. *"Turn jumbee."*

"You've been given a gris-gris, child," Escoba says sternly, gently touching my shoulder. "Papa Legba seeks payment. Understand? You do bad gris-gris, gris-gris come back around. Yes? You know this. Bad gris-gris is from Hawthorne. From Abigail and half moon. But you're not with Abigail, you're mine, child. Not of dirt, nor bird, nor fire. Bird isn't your mambo. Neither is fire or water. Yours is snake. Or is all this trouble from that oungan?"

I have no idea what she's talking about. But she waits for a response.

"I don't know," I say.

"You have a gris-gris from a jumbee, Mambo Cadence, Mambo Escoba give gris-gris to Abigail," Escoba says with a nod. "Mambo Escoba makes this better. You're mine, child. I take care of Abigail. I rid her for you." She takes a silver necklace out of her dress. There's a large cross at the end of it. "By God."

A whole group of white-clothed figures, ten or more, are twirling around and around the fire with more fervor than ever. It's making me dizzy. Some are running straight through the high flames.

"Cast gris-gris on you, I cast gris-gris on her," Escoba says with a shrug. "Mambo Escoba helps what is mine, love."

I feel sick. I am choking. I remember a filthy woman in rags, with white eyes, choking and trying to kill me.

Escoba brings the yellow snake up to her lips and kisses the snake's head right before my eyes.

"Jumbee, jumbee," she says to the snake. "Shh. *Jumbee, jumbee, jumbee.* Not of air. Not of feather. Not of water. Not of fire. Of Earth. Gris-gris takes thy mind, child. Mambo Escoba returns it for Hawthorne. You and I. Not Abigail. No one else. When half moon helps you, remember. Not her. You are with Escoba, child. Not falcon nor half moon.

"*Jumbee met gris-gris nan you?*" Escoba cries, staring up into the night sky. "*Mwen met, gris-gris nan Abigail. Jumbee, jumbee. Turn jumbee.*"

Escoba takes her silver cross and lays it gently against my forehead.

"Leave this child now. Cast jumbee under the cross and grace of God. Please, Jesus, take this gris-gris away. Cast jumbee out and leave sin for Abigail. Say these words and goodbye gris-gris. Good riddance to her."

My eyes open from the pain of my whole body being dragged over rocks and stone. Bryce is looking down at me, looking so worried. I close my eyes tight.

"*Further away from the house!*" cries Kenosha. "*Quick! Take her away from the door. Away from the house!*"

"*We have to close the door on her!*" shouts Mira. "*We can't let her get out!*"

"The door's broken," says Bryce.

"Not if we cast over it," Mira replies. "It can be locked by magic."

My eyes flutter open. I see a cloud passing by the bright light of the full moon. So peaceful. And stars. Then a flash of lightning. But no thunder. It's tranquil. The lightning along the clouds soothes me.

"Astraeus," I whisper. "Samhain. Hecate."

"Help me with the door, Bryce!" shouts Damien. "I can't close it. She's too strong!"

"*Jumbee, jumbee.*" I whisper. "*Duppy jumbee. Hawthorne turn jumbee.*"

"What's she saying?" Maddie asks me, crouched over.

Wooden boards crash against the wall, over and over, as if weathering a hurricane or typhoon.

"What's she saying?"

"Hand her the book!" cries Kenosha. "My god, give it quick. Put *Broomstick* in her hands! She's casting!"

"Cast jumbee under the cross and grace of God," I whisper. *"Cast jumbee out. Poor child. Leave sin for Abigail. Good riddance."*

The door stops slamming.

All goes dark.

Am I at peace? Dead? Perhaps. Perhaps death is the calmest silence? The Summerland.

But I feel a hand squeeze mine.

Then I worry again.

I feel Bryce. And Maddie. My brother. Mira. My friends. I long for them.

"Poor child," I whisper. "Poor, poor Melanie."

8

———————

THE HOWLING

I open my eyes to piercing screams. The shouts seem to echo all around me. I find myself lying on my back on leaves and mud. The full moon is bright over me. The stars are clear. All the mist has left the forest. Then I see faces. Bryce. Maddie. Damien. Mira. All my friends and family are crouching around me looking so concerned.

"Cadence," Bryce says. "Cadence."

"She nearly killed you, Katie," Maddie says, shaking her head and wiping tears from her eyes. "She was trying to strangle you to death!"

It's raining. Even though the sky is totally clear, rain is falling on my face. That's so weird—no weirder, I suppose, than the house, but impossible. But then I realize the rain is my tears. Do you understand? I don't know why, but I feel terribly sad. Not scared. Sad. And I'm willing the woods to rain. Because what happened to that woman in there is absolutely terrible. Is that why Alondra has been so sad?

There's a roar of thunder followed by lightning.

"I'm so sorry, Melanie," I say, gazing back at the house over Maddie's shoulder. "I'm sorry."

"Why are you sorry for her?" asks Mira.

Beyond Mira's shoulder, I see a witch in a forest green cloak standing before the boarded-up door in the pouring rain. She's laying down stones. Then she raises her arms and chants something. It's Kenosha.

"She saved us," Maddie says, gesturing to her.

"She brought you away from the witch," Bryce says, shaking his head. "But she didn't save us, Maddie. Cadence did. Cadence said an incantation with her book that locked her inside."

"I feel so sorry for her, Bryce." I turn back to him. "What have the witches done? The trap was laid by Melanie to take Alondra and Kenosha down in revenge. We were just a part of their plan. Even Enora. But Escoba could save me because I was guiltless. We all were."

"I don't understand," Bryce says, squeezing my hand and shaking his head.

"You don't need to. It's over."

But just then I hear howling in the rain again. And a woman screams repeatedly from inside the house.

"All that matters is that you're all right," Bryce says.

"I think I'm going to visit you more often, Firestarter," Mira quips, staring at the house. But then Courtney starts crying, and Mira walks over and hugs her.

"It's over," I repeat, reaching for Bryce's arm. He embraces me.

The rain stops.

Kenosha walks over to me. She's decked out in her green cloak, with her face dripping wet, moonlight shining over her many necklaces and earrings and water dripping from her bald head. She looks more like a witch than ever.

"Are you all right, Cadence?" Kenosha touches my forehead with her palm, then she looks back at the house. "I didn't want this to happen to you. I warned you."

"You came?"

"I had every wish to stay far away. When it was clear to me you thought your teacher was summoning you, I had to prepare. I left the house and did all I could to be ready for Samhain."

"Samhain, like Halloween?" asks Maddie.

"No, Madison," Kenosha says. "The Samhain Witch. A true Abaddon witch is here, one who's given her soul and everything to evil. The purest evil. There's no humanity left here. This time of the year in our pentacle provides her greatest power from the supernatural and is her time of vengeance. She's spent a lifetime learning the arts of Selene, not to be one with nature but to hurt Alondra and me. But she's mad. She's bent on hurting not only me but every member of the witch council. Even Enora. Any witch with any power. But her greatest desire is to hurt Alondra and me. When Alondra left us, I thought my casting was enough of a shield. Now I realize the Andromeda Witch and I, and now you, Windstorm, must prepare next year upon Mabon. We must prepare and keep her from hunting us."

There's a wail again. It's unnaturally loud, reverberating through the trees from the structure that was once a house. It echoes everywhere. Then I hear slamming, like doors and shutters closing, and animal grunting.

"You trapped her," Kenosha says, cocking her head back. "Only with Escoba's book. You trapped her, just as she trapped you by making you believe Alondra spoke to you."

"No, Alondra did speak to me, Kenosha," I say, shaking my head. "I'm sure of it. This wasn't a trap. I think, for some reason, Alondra wanted me here. So did *Broomstick*. She wanted me to see Melanie. Maybe Alondra is trapped in our world because of all this."

I stand up. All my friends look at me so oddly because a moment ago it probably looked like I didn't have the strength to raise my head. But I feel magic. A trance. My power is returning.

"I feel so sorry for her, Kenosha. We have to find a way to help her. God, she's broken. She's as confused as we are." That makes me want to cry again. I gaze up as a cloud drifts by the full moon in the clear sky. "Oh, Alondra, what did you do?"

"We have to go, babe," Bryce says, quietly touching my shoulder.

But then there's another torrent of screams. This time, it sounds like more than just Melanie. Maybe her mother? And then a crash. It sounds like something was thrown downstairs again. Or a wall is caving in.

"Your casting is strong," Kenosha says with a nod, "but it won't last. The witch's rage cannot be locked up this close to the house. Her hallowed ground, no doubt, extends beyond the house. We must move further into the woods, away from the house, before she escapes."

There's a howl as if from a wolf. And then a pack of animals—wolves?—fighting. Then the sound of fluttering bird wings. It all stops with another woman's scream.

"Please, Katie, let's get out of here," Maddie says, touching my shoulder.

9

LILIAS ADIE

It's a clear day with only a few wisps of clouds around a golden sun. Sometimes during this season between Mabon and Yule, Hawthorne isn't too hot or cold. That's what today is like. Down the hill is a nice manicured green lawn—it's fake and manmade, but I can still appreciate its beauty, even though I'm a witch. But the best part of everything on campus is the autumn colors. The trees surrounding our grassy hill, even trees along the main drag of campus, are covered in red and brown leaves. So I chose this table on our library patio, topped by a burgundy umbrella, to sit down with my study group and go over my hubby's recent lecture.

The students brought over a few chairs, because all ten of us can't fit by the table. And, god, hate to say it, but I'm getting old. I mean these students look like teenagers.

I love study groups. I mean Bryce gave me free rein to teach them any way I want. So it's fun planning them. Only last night I didn't have time to prepare. Their professor had to drum up some old material too. But I happen to know a lot about witches, so I'll make do.

"Let's talk about Lilias Adie, guys," I say. "Lilias was a sixty-year-old woman in Scotland wrongly accused by a neighbor of being a witch. Many of you see caricatures of witches as old and ugly. Like Mother Shipton. But actually it was easy for the justice system to accuse any woman of evil and working with the devil back then. And if you were frail, you couldn't do much to combat it. Well, what's truly heinous was her burial. Any of you guys know what was done to her body? Bryce...I mean, Dr. Wallace, will want you to know for the test."

"She was buried on the shore under the waves, Ms. Wallace," says Tiffany, a blonde girl in a T-shirt and shorts. "Between the tides. In Scotland, they didn't want to bury her in a blessed cemetery."

"Right, Tiffany. Why'd they do that?"

"The idea was that it was not a proper burial. It was totally disrespectful. Which was terrible if she was wrongfully accused."

"Yes," I say with a nod. I push the glasses back against my eyes. (All right, laugh it up, but Teacher Assistant Cadence Wallace has been reading a bit too many books lately and is wearing glasses now. Let's not talk about it.) "The burial was terrible, even more heinous for someone wrongfully accused. Women were mistreated and abused a lot back then." I look up pensively and then say, "But, tell me guys, would the sentence be wrong if Lilias was *rightfully* accused? What if she really did have sex with the devil? What if she really was a satanic sinner? Would she then deserve to have her body buried between tides? To never rest in peace? To wander the earth stuck between heaven and hell, like good 'ole Halloween's Stingy Jack, without a proper burial?"

"Yeah," a few say emphatically. Others just nod.

It's then that I spot a black-cloaked figure standing between brick buildings. Students walk right through her body. Her dark hood is over her head. No one else notices her. I do. And I know exactly who my favorite wicked witch standing there is.

THE END

CANDY CRONE

1

TOTALLY NOT SANTA

I CAN'T DECIDE WHICH IS BETTER. A PEPPERMINT STICK IN A STEAMY MUG OF cocoa, with tiny chocolate chips and thick chocolate syrup coating whipped cream, *OR* a cinnamon quill dipped in spicy bright red sauce and swirled caramel over vanilla ice cream in a large frosted silver bowl. I mean, they're both absolute bliss, right? The kick from the caramel apple surprise tastes good—*yum*—but that hot cocoa with the frosty whip is damn good too. So... I mean... I just don't know. My sweetest friend Frida introduced me to this caramel confectionery masterpiece last year, and I've been enjoying it ever since. Honestly, I think they're both to die for.

Whiffs of steam from the hot cocoa warm my face beside this large icy window looking out at all the trees in the surrounding wilderness. No one's walking along the one-way street through the frigid wind and icy snow tonight. Fluffy white blankets of snow coat the sides of the road, and ice flurries are blizzarding. The fresh snow reminds me of my vanilla ice cream. *Ummmm. Yummy.* It is sublime. Yep, I'm at Hawthorne Sweets again. But when I proposed meeting with this prospective student, I had no idea the weather would be so frigidly "anti-ice-cream."

I clutch my red jacket tighter over two layers of sweaters and jeans. *Brr*, it's cold. The weather is so unpredictable in Hawthorne, Georgia, you know. It didn't snow much at all last year.

"Cadence, Dad's fine with the idea now," Cat says across from me in the peach vinyl booth. "I'm telling you, he's fine with me going to college here in Hawthorne."

Do you remember Cat? She's that really fun teenager with pigtails on one side of her head and the other side bald that I met when going on a haunted haunt last year. Well, right now she's growing her hair out. Because she's applying to schools and has an important interview tomorrow. She'd almost look normal, if it weren't for the Gothic makeup. (Who am I to talk? I've got plenty of witchy makeup over my eyes and lips.) And...wait a second, just let me try another dip of this hot red sauce—I mean, shit, it's incredible.

Hawthorne Sweets is so surreal. All the walls on one side of this ice cream parlor are windowed. The other side is painted bright peach, pink, and white. And having this place a block away from my school, in the middle of the forest, is unreal. Not to mention that this season there are a bunch of large peppermint sticks and reindeer decals stuck on the walls. Two waitresses wearing cute peach-colored aprons and red-and-white elf hats are scooping ice cream behind a counter lined with classic silver stools. The place has a distinctive two-columned ice cream cone entrance. But tonight, the ice cream cone statues are covered in balsam fir and a shiny silver wreath with red and green lights. The silver tabletops are decorated for the season with reindeer placemats—mine has a glowing red nose. Until I learned about all our witchy occult secrets, it was a mystery to me why Hawthorne didn't celebrate Christmas. Well, not here at Hawthorne Sweets. Hawthorne Sweets is totally Santa.

"You're right, Cadence," Cat says, spooning luscious chocolate syrupy goo. "This ice cream here is really good."

"Sure is, Cat. Sure is." I swirl some red sauce and vanilla.

"After what happened at the Billington House," Cat says with a mouth full, "dad wants me to come to school here too."

"You gotta think of your studies," I say, shaking my head and laughing. "Your future's what's important, Cat, not magic stuff in Hawthorne. And they might not even accept you here."

"My grades are good enough. The interview isn't about getting in, it's all about the scholarship. I'm already in Hawthorne."

"You're meeting with Dr. Kahn?" I sip my hot cocoa. Then I rub my protruding belly thinking of my unborn baby, Chandra. This stuff is great and all, but I might be looking at quite a bellyache for me and you, darling. "Dr. Kahn's a good history professor, one of my favorites. Just talk to him about the Shang dynasty." I swirl my spoon in the red sauce and lick it. "He's fascinated by China. Talk about Confucius. Maybe . . ." I wag my silver spoon at her in thought. "Throw in some Confucian philosophy stuff."

"See, Cadence, you're already helping."

"Well, if you're accepted, you can't join my coven. I already have twelve sisters."

"Cadence!" She grunts and hits the table. "Why not?"

"The circle's complete," I say with a shrug. "Forget witchcraft and just focus on your studies."

"Sweets for little children to eats?"

What the hell? The words are jarring coming from a pale, wrinkled lady shuffling down the row of booths, repeating the words over and over again.

"Sweets for children to eat? Sweets for children to eats?"

She's wearing a raggedy earthy-brown sweater over a gray dress and a black cloth headdress. There's a mark on her long nose. Like a wart. I've seen this lady rummaging through the trash cans on campus. I didn't think much of it then, but right now, crouched over and squinting at us, she looks like your classic image of a witch.

She's going by each booth handing people small candy canes in plastic wraps.

"Growly, growler," she keeps muttering while handing out treats to kids. "Growly, growler."

She stops by a booth behind Cat with two kids and their mom.

"Sweets for children to eats?" she asks again with a chuckle. "Hmm? Make 'em plump. Make 'em strong. So they may run, run, run along."

The boy and girl lurch back. Then the old lady raises a finger, digs in a pocket in her dress, and thrusts more small candy canes toward them.

"Would you care for one, my little one?" she asks the boy. Then she turns to the little girl. "And my, my, what's your name, child?"

"Miley," squeaks the kid.

"Miley? Such a name. Stout. Strong. Have you been good? Have you been behaving?" The hag leans a bit too close to Miley's face. "Being nice for... *Santy Claus*?" Then she explodes into laughter. The little girl nods her head nervously while her mom glares at the crone. "'Tis the Yule season of joy. There'll be no Krampus for you. Krampus runs with his birch rods punishing naughty children, he does. But there will be no Krampus for you."

The little girl shyly nods her head again.

"Would you like to try one?"

The girl nods and reaches over, but her mom snatches her hand.

"No, thank you," says the mother. Then she shakes her head at her daughter. "Miley, no. You have your ice cream."

"Growly, growler," says the old woman, tossing another two small plastic bags on their table. "Growly, growler."

She shrugs and walks on.

Oh no. Our booth's next.

"How about you?" the woman asks us. "But...oh my!" She opens her eyes wide and points at my belly. "Appears you've been eating a bit too many sweets already, child."

"I'm pregnant," I say.

"Pregnant?" she says with a grimace. Then she opens her eyes wide. "Pregnant? And at such a wondrous time." She extends her arms, looking up at the ceiling. "Some parts, ole St. Nicholas has his competition on this night, he does. Others far in the North, by the North Pole, see so many people rushing through the streets laughing and swatting all the kids' asses. They parade in groups under smoke and fire wearing the heads of goats. Rushing down the streets in horns and fur baring sharp teeth. But not here. No, no, not here. No birch rod where all the children are nice and so well behaved. No birch rod whipping for you."

She offers me and Cat two small candy canes in plastic wrappers. We take them just to be polite. I'm a bit repulsed glancing at the old lady's fingers with all that dirt and muck on her skin.

Cat reaches into her small purse and hands a few dollars to the old woman. The woman becomes too cheery, opening her eyes wide.

"Oh, my, oh my! Bless you! Bless you, child. No birch rod for you!"

Then the hag roars with laughter again. And she reaches into her dress and hands Cat a large chocolate cookie. It actually looks like a fresh chocolate chip brownie cookie, but I'm guessing Cat isn't about to take a bite, as bewildered as I am as to where the old lady got it from.

"Excuse me, miss," says one of the waitresses behind her.

"Yes, dearie?" the old hag cocks her head back.

"You can't offer people food in our restaurant."

"Why? On such an upstanding evening?" She puts her finger to her lips. "Tonight he comes. He comes, shh...the goat comes bringing cookies and cakes and candy to all the lucky boys and girls. And they enjoy it so. Just to bring a smile to the little ones' lips. But . . . don't be naughty." She turns and looks deeply into my eyes. A dark shadow is cast over her. It feels cold. "Woe to those who are naughty. He swats them. He takes his birch sticks out and hits 'em. And what do you think we do out here to kids misbehaving in the woods? Grýla stirs her pot. Boil boggled and broggled. Fresh and plump. I keep the pot nice and warm for all those naughty, naughty little children."

"Sweets for children to eats!" she calls out again, continuing farther down the aisle. "Sweets for children to eats." And then more quietly, under her breath, she keeps repeating, "growly growler. Growly growler."

She tosses more candy canes on a couple's table by the exit and then, thankfully, exits out the door.

"She was weird," Cat says.

She sure was. That's how weird it gets in Hawthorne, I suppose. I've seen even stranger. But, as usual, Cat's the kind of person who hardly minds; she's grinning, seemingly loving it. That's Cat. She and her father have been ghost hunting all her life. She lives for weird stuff like this.

But she moves the old crone's chocolate cookie very far from her dish, near the napkin dispenser.

"Tell me more about Doctor Kahn, Cadence. I told you, I'm here no matter what, and you can't convince me otherwise. Even if you don't let me into your coven. But I need more gems for my interview tomorrow."

I dip my spoon in my ice cream. Then I take a swig of hot chocolate.

"Hmm?" I ask, chewing on a chocolate chip. "I only had one class with him, but Maddie had a few. You should ask Maddie. I think . . . he also lectures a lot about the Han dynasty. Chinese history is his specialty. Look a little into ancient China tonight. I heard he likes to emphasize the impact of this dynasty in the development of China's organization and government. So, I'd—"

There's a high-pitched scream. It's from the booth closest to the exit. Then I hear cackling from that weird woman again, this time right outside the window. The hag rushes by our window, clutching her head-dress tightly over her head, as ice and wind blow hard against her face.

Cat jumps. "Eww! Look, Cadence!" She points at the small plastic wrappers that woman gave us, only there aren't any candy canes. The candy canes have been transformed into squiggly brown worms, rubbing against the clear plastic wrappers.

"Oh, gross! Look!" Cat points at the cookie.

The cookie that crone handed Cat is now just a small mound of mud with white maggots wiggling around and a couple flies swarming it.

There's crying. It's coming from the booth behind Cat. It's the little girl.

"Mommy, my stomach hurts."

2

HAPPY HALLOWEEN

"Be gentle, Cadence," my best friend Maddie warns. We make our way up a paved walkway. There's a brick facade on the front of the single-story home. Maddie and I are wearing thick, heavy coats, and the path leading to the front door is lined by fluffy white snow, covering the bushes and grass. It's not as stormy anymore, but it's really cold. "If she carries on, just let her keep talking. Don't challenge what she says. And don't jump in talking about the candy canes. You haven't seen her since Mom's wedding, and she's still real confused." Then she lifts a hand, ready to knock, but first turns to me. "Be slow and be patient. And . . . whatever you do, don't talk about witches, okay?"

"How am I going to mention the other night if I can't talk about witches, Maddie?"

"Well, I told you that you shouldn't come if you're just here to get information from her. She might be confused, but she's sharp, as bright as you. Maybe hint, but don't be direct. She can't take talking about witchcraft. If you get her too angry, well, she won't fight you with magic, but she'll clam up. She didn't say a word or eat for three days after Mom last mentioned Geneva Forest. So . . . are you ready?"

"Not after your telling me all this."

"You'll be fine," Maddie says with a chuckle, touching my arm. "She loves it when Mom and I come and visit. I think she'll love seeing you. I mean, she wouldn't be here if it weren't for you."

An older woman with long red hair and glasses opens the door. We remove our thick coats and put them on hooks by the door. Then we take off our boots, wet with ice. Inside, the place is warm. It smells like chicken soup. It's dark even though most of the drapes are open. I think the darkness is because it's cloudy outside. We pass a lady with a yellow-dyed crew cut and rings on her nose and lips watching TV near the kitchen. A disheveled lady is pacing back and forth by a saffron-curtained window, wearing a T-shirt and sweatpants. Then we pass a room with a woman in gray sweatpants and a T-shirt on the carpet brushing paint on a canvas. I peek at the painting. It's a lady in a long black dress and tall black hat sitting beside a cat. The artwork is a bit strange, but really good. Finally, in the room at the end of the hall, a figure with long golden-blond hair in light blue pajamas is sitting in a fluffy brown corduroy lounge chair. There's an open bag of chips lying on the floor, a few stray tortilla chips, and a bunch of lit candles on a table with a tray of uneaten food. She's just staring through the window.

"Hi, Melanie," Maddie says.

"Hi, Madison," Melanie mutters. She still stares, but her lips curl into a smile. "Hi, Cadence. So nice for you to visit me. Happy Halloween."

"Merry Christmas, Melanie," Maddie corrects. "How are you doing?" She reaches down and hugs her. "Mom found some work for you near Pooler. We thought getting you a job might help you feel a little better. Or did you start work at the local laundromat? That's just down the street, right?"

"Aha," Melanie says. "See. I already started quilting." She points to the blanket over her body. "I love sewing. First thing I ever sewed was Winnie's stomach. When her doll was all flayed open, I tied the skin real taut. Remember, Momma?"

She finally breaks her stare and looks at me.

"Sure, Melanie. Sure."

"You're not my momma," Melanie snarls, shaking her head.

But then she weirdly reaches out for me to hug her.

"It's nice to see you again," Melanie says in my embrace. "How are you, Cadence?"

"I'm fine, Melanie. Fine. You're doing okay?"

"Things are nice. Very nice. But things aren't going so well back home in Hawthorne I hear?"

"No, everything is fine."

Melanie shakes her head.

"Cadence just wanted to visit with me this time," Maddie says.

"You, Madison, maybe, but not her. Why would Kathy come all the way through the cold snow to see me? Bonnie tells me she ain't never remembered the roads being this icy. Lammas was colder than ever. What's happening with the weather lately? I think God's planning some sort of punishment. I think the heat changing to cold means something's going on with God. God's probably fighting Satan again. God's always fighting Satan. It probably means the first break of the seals. Of course, it's warm inside, isn't it? Thanks to God."

She smiles and buries her head in her hands. Then she starts shaking. *Is she laughing?* Maddie glances at me, flashing a rueful grin.

Melanie, once called the Samhain Witch, was the most powerful witch in the world. The witch council couldn't control her. Neither could my mentor witch, Alondra. It was only when I developed the talent of seeing demons—something I'd rather not have seen—that I helped her. That's when she nearly choked me to death.

Did I help her? According to Madison and Aunt Jane, she spends all her time just sitting by this window. Maybe she would have been better off living like Bigfoot, as her muddy, smelly self under the shelter of mud and leaves in our forest?

"Been cryin' lately?" Melanie asks me. She lifts those black eyes, gazing right into mine, reminding me of her ego witch-self. I quickly shake my head. "People never stop their crying. They cry and cry and cry. But they never really stop crying. Even after babies grow, the tears never stop falling. They still cry." Thankfully, she breaks her gaze. "When I was little, Winona used to cry a lot. Mommy sure would get upset at all of her crying. You know what I'd say? I'd say—wagging my finger—'now, Winnie, you do what Momma tells you or else. No use cryin' all the time.' And she knew what I meant, she sure did. She never crossed me after I learned how to play with black stars and crosses. You can always take sticks from those sigils and stop everybody from crying."

Maddie nods, standing over her, forcing an uncomfortable grin.

"Back when all the other kids went playing with fire trucks, riding bikes or playing with boards, Winnie and I would go out with our special deck of cards. I'd rummage through the cards giving everyone a reading. Got to the time when I was pretty darn good at playing cards. Got to be that it always came true. Everything. I'm really good at playing cards, Cadence. That's why I know you're not just visiting to see me. You understand, sometimes a flush is a flush, a full house is a full house, and it just ain't worth nothin' bettin' too much money when you're destined to lose. Just like it ain't worth nothin' to try to stop folks from crying. They still cry. But Winona and Daddy always lost when betting cards against me. Because I was pretty good, and I didn't cry so much back then. Remember, Momma?"

She weirdly looks up at me again as if I'm her mom.

She's so weird. Her body looks so delicate and thin in her blue pajamas and with that blanket over her body—but not her eyes. Those eyes are terrifying. The obsidian orbs gaze right into you. Intelligent, just like Maddie said, but menacing. She might be rambling like a lunatic, but I feel like there's a part of her that's ready to lash out and tear my throat out again. But, even creepier, she also seems ready to burst into laughter.

Is she talking nonsense? Genius? I'm not sure. All I know is she scares the hell out of me.

Her eyes turn vacant. But because she keeps looking at me, I hesitantly shake my head again.

"It was hard for Mom and Dad and my sister when I was little," she says with a nod, looking back to the window. "It's hard to stop the crying. The crying really never ends until you're under dirt, and then, well . . . you just can't hear them tears fall anymore."

She grips her head in her hands, and her whole body shakes again.

"Melanie," I say hesitantly. "I came because I wanted to ask you about Christmas. There's a Christmas witch that did a curse at an ice cream parlor, seeming to hurt a little girl. Do you know of an old witch that attacks children during the Christmas season? When you haunted Halloween, did another witch haunt Christmas afterward? This witch referred to herself as *Grýla*, like the Icelandic witch. I asked Kenosha, but she was unsure."

Melanie freezes with her head still in her hands. Then she quickly shakes—not just her head, her whole body.

"No, Kates," Maddie mutters quietly, shaking her head. "No, not now."

"A Yule witch, or—"

"Help yourselves to eating," Melanie says, looking up with a big smile. Then she stretches out her arms and yawns. She gestures to a sandwich on a paper plate on the table as if no one said anything. "They always make me bologna sandwiches for lunch. I mean, you can add mustard, but, I mean, come on. Bologna sandwiches? Just plain white bread and bologna and they call that lunch. I told Bonnie time and time again that I fuckin' hate bologna, but there it is. Just as there be bologna in Hawthorne, there be bologna in my goddamn bedroom. See?"

"This witch is turning candy into worms," I add.

Melanie quickly shakes her head. But I stop talking when Melanie buries her head in her hands again.

"No, Cadence," Maddie snaps. "No."

"Melanie," Maddie drawls, taking a knee beside her chair and gently touching her shoulder. "Why don't we go over your money arrangements? Mom and I are going to help you get an account."

Melanie looks up. "But I don't have any money, Madison," she says with tears running down her cheeks. She looks so sad.

"I know," Maddie says, "I know. But you will. You said you're working at the laundromat. We should discuss financial arrangements."

"I was only joking about all that," she says with a laugh. "I'm not working in the laundromat."

"Well . . . you're going to start work soon," Maddie says. "And when you do, you're going to need to be saving."

"You're so nice."

"Willow suggested . . ." I continue.

"Stop it, Cadence!" Maddie snaps. "Shut up! What did I tell you?"

"A child was hurt by magic, Maddie," I object. "That little girl looked like her stomach was in pain after eating the worm."

"Ever cut open a stomach?" Melanie asks. "Get plenty of worms that way. Worms and blood and a horrible smell. They're all there underneath the skin, muscles, and bones, if you take a look. Not really something anybody bothers to talk about, not even doctors. It's like smashing pumpkins and tearing out all that sinew and pumpkin. But I'd rather not talk about worms and ice cream. Please tell her to stop talking about worms and ice cream, Madison."

"Never mind, Melanie," Maddie says gently. "Never mind." Then Madison looks up at me, seeming ready to slug me. "Mom and I are planning to get you an account. So I think that. . ."

I grip my hand tightly. But then. . . I venture to the window.

It's pleasant watching the snowflakes slowly fall outside. A table on a small concrete patio is now covered in a blanket of snow. Beyond a bunch of old suburban houses is a small park with a bunch of trees with hanging moss. I love Spanish moss on trees. It makes Savannah so pretty. I remember Kenosha talking about the trees in New Orleans that have moss like that. Hawthorne is too far up in elevation to have trees like that.

"Growly, growler," Melanie says.

I whirl around.

"What did you say?" I snap. "That's what that witch said in the ice cream parlor."

"What?" Melanie asks.

"*Growly, growler.* You said *growly, growler.*"

"But she won't be bothering your nice friends," Melanie says. "Your friends are all grown up. That handsome husband of yours, Bryce, and your brother, Damien. Even Madison's mom and your nice dad. All the old people are safe. They cry a lot, but they keep it all inside. That's of no use for Yule. But not a child. Or a newborn baby. They're just ripe enough. And you're beginning to show, aren't you, Cadence? That could be something."

"Is Grýla going to threaten my baby, Melanie?"

When she turns to the window ready to go mum again, it's too much. I rush right over and turn her toward me. She stares at my hands, which are holding her. A flicker of rage erupts on her face. In a flash, I'm reminded of how dangerous she is.

"It's not fair," Melanie drawls, still staring at my hands, "when they want to take something so cute and cuddly, so sweet, and turn it sour."

"What's she going to do to my baby? What, Melanie? What are you talking about? You said '*growly, growler.*' How did you know that phrase?"

"Well . . . Yuletide . . . is a cold time, Windstorm. Over the years, hope was always that crops and wheat would grow so people wouldn't starve to death. That's why we celebrate the light at the end of the maze. Anyone who wishes to get the energies during this part of the year is going to be feeding on children in preparation for Imbolc. They're looking for fire to light the lampshade. Sometimes seven candles will do, other times, just one, the one in the center of your chest. Like you and your baby, Chandra."

"How do you know my baby's name!"

She's freaking me out. I feel panicked. Maddie's looking worried now too.

"I'm just saying, it's not all about stockings and candy and fat, jolly gremlins making their way down chimneys eating cookies and handing out gifts. It's that feeling you get. It's that nice warm baby-fresh feeling. Like smelly diapers and pee. Just like your friend Madison here."

"You've never heard of a Christmas witch this time of year?"

"I *sure* don't want to be talking about witches."

"But how did you know that phrase: *growly, growler*?"

"Madison sure is right," Melanie says, weirdly opening her eyes wide, "I sure don't like talking about witches." She smiles and touches my hand. "You know, Olivia and Tiffany are such friendly roommates. Did you meet them? Tiffany's a really good drawer. She loves drawing. Ask her to draw something for you. She drew me a drawing of me sitting in this chair when it was clear and sunny outside. It was so pretty. And she drew another of a vase and flowers. Isn't that great? Just a vase with flowers. She called it a . . . still life. I don't understand why people like drawing dead flowers, but they sure are pretty. And why is it called still life? Cause it's still? Like dead? Did she show you her art with dead flowers? Ask Tiffany to draw one of her dead flowers for you. And Olivia, well, she makes me laugh—"

"Melanie, is Grýla going to hurt Chandra?"

"Selfish," Melanie snaps, turning back to the window. She folds her arms. "Don't like talking about witches. *Navitas Nativitatis. Navitas Nativitatis. Navitas Nativitatis. Per dominum. Per dominum.* What more can I say? It's like tarot. All this talk about witches leads to witchcraft. Then you fight witches with witchcraft, and magic makes witches turn to witches. Which you apparently wish a witch to be? Stop all your crying." She shakes her head. "Be brave. I never really thought there could be good witches in the world, but when you helped me, Cadence, I saw you were a good witch. So are you, Madison. So is your mom. I like you witches. If it wasn't for you, I would still be left out in the cold."

"We like you too, Melanie," Maddie says. "She'll stop talking about all this. *Won't you*, Cadence?"

"But . . . does she want—"

"Which or witches. Spells spell spells."

"Melanie," Maddie says. "We just want you to be well."

"But Melanie—"

Melanie turns to me with a blank stare. She looks confused. While Maddie looks angrier at me than ever. So . . . I lose my nerve.

"It's," I say with a sigh, "it's really good seeing you again, Melanie."

"So nice for you to visit me, Cadence. Happy Halloween."

3

WITCH HUNTING

BRYCE AND I PASS BETWEEN THAT TWO-COLUMNED ENTRANCE WITH ICE cream statues, converted to giant Christmas trees, by the entrance to Hawthorne Sweets. Mira and Kenosha aren't far behind. I glance back at them; they look so intense. That makes me laugh. Hey, what do you get when four witches walk into an ice cream bar ready to open up a can of witch whoop ass? Either a real bad joke or a gunslinging paranormal movie. I know we're worried about this new witch in town, but walking into an ice cream parlor ready for a magic brawl seems silly.

Mira raises her eyebrows at me. But Bryce gets my mirth, smiling. So I take my hubby's hand.

We are passing two peach vinyl booths full of college students blissfully gorging on ice cream. It's late, so the other booths are empty.

"Hi, Doctor Trent," a student says to Kenosha.

"Oh, hello, Owen," says Kenosha with a smile. Kenosha's wearing a wig and looks professorly, instead of like a bald witch, because we're only a block away from campus.

"Hi, Professor Wallace," says another boy in a red Hawthorne sweater.

"Hi, Kai," Bryce says.

I head over to a middle-aged lady wearing a red felt hat with a white pom-pom and a peach dress and apron wiping down a silver stool. She was here when Cat and I ate here last time.

"Excuse me, miss? Do you remember that elderly woman stopping by here offering people candy canes?"

"Yes. I told her she can't hand out food to our customers."

"Has she been back?" asks Kenosha.

"No, thank goodness. She left a trail of trash. Would you all like a booth? You can take any open table you'd like."

"Which table were you sitting at, Cadence?" asks Kenosha.

I point to a now-vacant booth. And we sit in the same place I sat with Cat, only this time Bryce is beside me and Kenosha and Mira are across from us. Then I grab one of the laminated menus leaning by the napkin dispenser. It's usually the same large pictures of those same incredible sundaes but, this month, it's full of hollies and fir leaves and pictures of Santa Claus and his reindeer.

"Where on the table was the transmutation?" asks Kenosha.

"The candy canes were by our ice cream bowls," I say, putting a finger on my chin. "And the cookie . . . I think, well . . . I'm sure Cat's cookie turned into mud right there by the window."

"*Revelare*," Mira says with a nod, closing her eyes and running her fingers near the napkin holder. "*Revelare*. Reveal the Christmas witch."

"Christmas witch, Mira?" I laugh. "I thought the circle agreed on Grýla?"

"Cadence, stop laughing at all this," Mira says. "Afreyea arranged this investigation for the council."

"Sorry," I say with a shrug. "I just think *Christmas Witch* sounds funny."

"Why has your circle decided on calling this witch Grýla, Cadence?" Kenosha asks.

But my cellphone rings in my small purse before I can reply. I dig in the bag and look. It's Raymond, Cat's dad. He's probably checking on how my meeting with his daughter went. But before I can answer, the call drops.

"We have to call her something," Bryce says with a shrug. "Legend has it that Grýla disguised herself as a beggar in order to gather up the naughty children to boil in her pot. It fits Katie's description. That old lady was up to no good with the kids. And the witch even called herself by that name, Kates said. She said she stirs a pot for naughty children."

"And she kept saying '*Growly, growler*,'" I say with a nod. "It was weird coming from a normally quiet homeless woman wandering campus. It's like she was acting more like a witch than even the Samhain Witch. This witch is old and wears tattered clothing. She's even got a wart on her nose. I mean, Melanie was covered in mud, which was terrifying enough, but this lady looks *textbook* witch."

"What about our former Halloween Witch?" asks Kenosha. "Did the Samhain Witch have any idea what all this was about?"

"A whole lot of nothing. Melanie rambled on and on, talking nonsense. She's crazy. But at one point, Melanie said *growly, growler*. That got my attention. When I pressed her on it, she said all my sisters were safe, but she hinted that the witch might go after my unborn baby. I kept asking her about that—'cause that totally freaked me out—but she wouldn't explain much further. Or at least she didn't say anything else that made much sense. The only thing I could make out was Melanie talking about energies during this Christmas season, dark energies, that grow by feeding on children."

"Grýla is just an Icelandic myth, Windstorm," Mira says. "It's folklore."

"But it sounds like our witch knows the folklore too," objects Kenosha, nodding pensively. Then Kenosha weirdly closes her eyes and runs her fingers over the table. She breathes in and out, focusing deeply, like Mira did before.

"Did you all decide on something?" asks the waitress.

"I'll have your caramel apple surprise," I say. "Maybe with some extra red hot syrup. It's so good."

"Two spoons," Bryce says to the waitress, lifting two fingers.

The waitress looks at Mira and Kenosha. After Kenosha bobs her head up and down a few times with her eyes closed, the waitress gets the hint and leaves.

"I don't feel anything," Kenosha says finally, heaving a sigh.

"Well, the ice cream here is amazing," I say, putting my menu back behind the dispenser. "You should really try some, Kenosha. Chandra loves it. When I taste sugar, she goes crazy in my belly."

"Did you see any demons around the witch?" Kenosha asks me.

"Samhain or Grýla?"

"Either."

"I always see demons." But then I remember seeing a shadow cover Grýla. "Yes . . . when the witch met my gaze standing over this booth, a shadow was cast over her. Yeah, demons were behind her. She felt very evil."

"How about now?"

I really don't want to. Necromancy is a talent I never wanted. The only other witch I know that can see demons like I can is Melanie, and look what the talent did to her.

See that black shade lying flat against the wall as if he's just a leftover Halloween prop? You might mistake him for a torn old costume if it weren't for his bright white eyes. There's another bunched up on the ceiling by the door. They never move. The only things that stir are their shredded, tattered bodies as they flutter like flags in the wind.

"They're here," I say. "So, Kenosha?"

"Are there more in this restaurant than usual?" asks Kenosha.

"No."

"You said that you had a dream after the transmutation?" asks Kenosha. "Like a witch wandering, Cadence?"

"In my dream," I reply thoughtfully with a nod, "I thought I was in another witch wandering. I was walking in the dark forest around my house. Snow was on the ground, but I felt warm, even though I had disrobed. I . . . I felt threatened. Usually in my wanderings, I feel empowered. Not in this dream. That's what made me feel like I was being hunted. When I started feeling too creeped out, I stopped and hunted for large sticks and branches. I piled them one on top of another and formed the shape of a pentagram, then glided a stick in the mud creating a circle around it. That was weird. I have no idea why I did that. And, weirder, all the while, I kept hearing babies crying."

"It sounds like you were casting a shield spell," Kenosha suggests.

"You might have been protecting against oneiromancy," Mira says. "This witch might have been attacking you in your dreams, Cadence, like Enora and Melanie once did."

"But the strangest thing is Cadence and I have seen this homeless woman rummaging through trash cans on campus," Bryce says. "Katie's description perfectly matches the lady. If it's the same woman, that old lady is harmless. She minds her own business."

"That's why I asked about demons, Bryce," suggests Kenosha. "It could be a demon possession."

"You thought Cadence was possessed," he objects.

"In a way, she was," Kenosha says. "By achieving mastery over her demons, Cadence was able to rid herself of Alondra's spirit. Melanie was possessed too. We all saw the Samhain Witch's transformation after Cadence defeated her. Part of her 'muddiness' left her."

The waitress comes over with my huge sundae. Wow, three huge scoops of vanilla ice cream are buried under all this hot red syrup, caramel, and chocolate chips. And the cinnamon stick is totally like the cherry on top. I think I could eat this every night. I don't have to worry so much about overeating being pregnant. Right?

But first, I pass the large frosty silver bowl to the love of my life. I watch Bryce take a spoonful of that spicy apple sauce over the vanilla ice cream. Then I do the same with the cinnamon stick, instead of a silver spoon. And it's . . . incredible. Wow. It's that perfect mix of spiciness, tart apple, and vanilla.

"The only magic I witnessed was the transformation of candy into worms," I say with my mouth full of ice cream. "That doesn't strike me as someone powerful like Melanie. But I contacted you guys after Cat and I saw the little girl's mom have to help her into the car that night. We were worried about the girl. You guys sure you don't want some ice cream? There's plenty. Frida got me to love this dish."

"Did you get a hint of the location in the forest in your dream?" Kenosha asks.

"No."

We turn pensive. Except Bryce. He's clanging his silver spoon against the silver dish, eating more of my amazing dessert.

"When I spoke with Afreyea, guys," Mira says, "the headmaster of the witch council was very worried. Something about the transmutation of candy bothered her. Even if all that witch is doing is terrifying little children and causing stomachaches, messing with kids is enough for us to get involved. Afreyea even suggested that she visit us from all the way over in Cotonou to investigate."

"Cadence, you're the Hawthorne Witch," Kenosha says to me. "It's your responsibility to keep this magic under control. We can't wait for Afreyea to travel here from Africa."

"I know," I say. "I don't want a witch in Hawthorne harming kids."

"We have to find her," Kenosha says with a nod, "and meet with her. See what she or her possessor desires. That's what our council's been doing for centuries with rogue witches. That's what I was asked to do with my Crescent coven when investigating Alondra years ago."

"I'll search the woods with you tonight," Mira says.

My phone buzzes, vibrating the purse by my hip. I pull it out again and silence the ringer.

"If it's a demon possession, we need to exorcise it," Kenosha adds. "If she's turned criminal, like Enora, we need to turn her over to the police. If insane, like Melanie, she needs help. Either way, we have to find her and stop this negative presence in Hawthorne."

I glance down at my phone; the contact reads *Raymond* again. A text message reads: *Emergency. Please answer.*

And the phone vibrates again.

"Ray?" I ask, putting my phone up to my ear.

"Cadence, Catrina's missing," Raymond blurts out. "I haven't heard from her since the day she arrived. Of course, Cat has her way of roaming for a day or two, but now I'm really worried. Did she tell you she might be staying somewhere else in Hawthorne?"

"No."

"That's what I was afraid of. I called the hotel and, even though I booked the room, they couldn't tell me much more due to privacy. You know Cat's crazy, but even when she left home and crossed the border into Mexico, she told me exactly where she was. She knows I worry. Her last words were that she was going into Hawthorne Forest to investigate some haunting. She texted it was the biggest supernatural thing she had ever seen. Did she tell you about something going on in Hawthorne Forest?"

"No."

He goes silent.

"My friends and I will do everything we can," I say.

"I'm driving down to Hawthorne now."

"You can stay at our house, Raymond."

I look over at Bryce. He nods.

"That'd be—" He takes a deep breath. "That'd be great, Cadence. Cat looks up to you so much. This time, it's more than a ghost investigation. It's my daughter. Her last message made no sense. It just read *growly, growler*. Do you have any idea what that means?"

I sure do. But before I can tell him, the phone goes dead. Though horrible timing, this isn't so unusual. It's happened many times before on the drive to our desolate college town.

I put my head in my hands and run my fingers through my long hair.

"What is it, Cadence?" Bryce asks, rubbing my back.

"She took Cat."

"Who?" asks Kenosha.

"Grýla."

"How do you know?" asks Mira.

"Cat's last text to her dad read *growly, growler*."

"Told you this was serious, Cadence," Mira says. "This isn't just about candy causing stomachaches."

"We've gotta find her. God, he said she told him she was heading into the forest to investigate. She's probably lost in Hawthorne Forest. If anything happens to Cat, I feel responsible. I only made her more excited about Hawthorne and witchcraft when I met her for that ghost haunting last year. If she's hurt, it'll be all my fault."

"That's nuts," Mira says. "None of this is your fault."

"We have to look for her tonight. Cat is out there in the cold."

"Hawthorne Forest is over a hundred square miles," Kenosha says, shaking her head. "Your friend is literally a needle in a haystack. I suggested Mira and I wander a little to look for this witch too, but I meant locally and with magic, and I thought weeks, even months, not days . . . I'll contact the council. Afreyea should come here."

"But you said it yourself, Kenosha. There's no time."

"Cadence, you can at least wait till morning," Kenosha objects. "Tomorrow morning. Not now. This is the coldest it's been all year and you're pregnant. You might dream walk in the forest at night, but you and your baby won't do well searching for real out there in the cold. Get rest. Mira and I can do more searching tonight around campus."

"I'll go too," Bryce says.

"If she's not near the college, we'll regroup with the entire coven in the morning," Kenosha says with a nod.

I'm staring down at my ice cream. Somehow this amazing red-and-white caramelly delight isn't so wonderful anymore.

"Will you, please, listen to me just this once, Cadence?" Kenosha asks.

I nod slowly.

The trees outside are in shadows in the dark night. It's not snowing, and the moon is shining through clouds, but I think of how bitingly cold it is, seeing all the ice still piled along the street. I will my eyes to see the dark demons. For Cat, I'll do that. Demons thrive in darkness, and right now they're all over the trees outside the window, in hiding. And that means they're all over the wilderness around Cat. One tall, lanky demon is creepily just standing on the street watching me with its creepy bright white eyes.

I jump when Bryce puts his arm around me. He flashes a rueful grin. So I lean my head on his shoulder.

"We have to find her, Bryce. We just have to."

4
____

MIDNIGHT BLUE

I'm slowly walking along a narrow street walled by three-story buildings where everything is shaded a midnight blue. Even the streetlights hanging down over me shine indigo. So many windows open into one another from across a teal cobblestone road.

The path winds, and I pass an adjoining street. Here water unnaturally flows very slowly from a large central stone fountain reflecting white-chocolate moonlight. And all is quiet—except for a baby crying.

On the next street, the moon is just bright enough to flash a glance at my own reflection on a shop window. I'm naked, but I feel warm. It's almost as if this dark blue is enough to clothe me. The street widens enough here for small tables and chairs to be laid out. All is still. Except the sound of a baby crying.

White light brightens across another fork in the road, and a large black cat crosses my path. It just stands still amidst the pale turquoise shade. Then the cat shakes, crouches down, and slowly lengthens into a large naked dark-skinned man. But before I can get a better look, the man darts off on all fours.

I pass a shop window revealing a lovely skirt and blouse on a faceless mannequin in front of rows of hangers. On the opposite side of the street is a café. Through the windows I see chairs leaning on empty tables inside dark halls.

I hear footsteps. Someone's following me.

I turn and a tall naked dark-skinned man is standing beside me with sapphire eyes gazing down into mine. Light blue, almost aqua, shines over his ripped chest, large arms, and broad shoulders. His eyes make me feel so calm. There is such warmth in his gaze. I let him run two fingers slowly along my cheek. The fingers wander over my lips, and I run my tongue along his fingers. They taste sweet, as if dipped in maple syrup. Then his fingers, now wet from my lips, run slowly down my neck and along the curve of my breast. Some of his syrup drips on my skin. He bends down and licks my nipple and then sucks my breast. And I embrace him too, desiring him. I want so much to kiss those lips again, to taste the sweetness, desiring that sugar, so I lift his head back and press those soft lips against mine. All the while his fingers probe, massaging deep into my skin, sliding down the slippery curves of my breasts and hips, down to my ass.

Cold stone presses along my back as I'm gently pushed against a hard wall. His eyes shine brighter. And under shining blue light, his torso now shines aqua.

He presses harder into me. His whole body, sticky and wet, as if bathed in molasses, pushes into me. With strong hands, he squeezes the crack of my ass. I reach down and run my fingers over hard muscular abs, while my other hand runs along the muscles over his back. He pinches my butt hard again, almost hurting me. I close my eyes and bring my lips back to his face, ravenously tasting all that sweet stickiness, licking syrupy sweat off his skin. He tastes so sweet. But then . . . my tongue feels fur.

I don't recall facial hair?

Opening my eyes, I can't see his face. His head has disappeared. But I feel something contract against my chest, heavy in my arms.

I'm holding a black cat!

I throw the cat off and he lands on his hind legs. He turns, raises his back, and hisses, then he darts off down an adjacent alley, like that man on all fours did before.

⁓

My eyes open to flickering candlelight surrounding my bed in my dark bedroom. I lit these candles when I focused all my intent to cast magic to help my friends. I was scrying to find Cat with dream magic. I asked Hecate to conjure a spell in my sleep to help find her in the forest by scrying. Seems I summoned the wrong cat.

5

ALONDRA'S OFFICE

It's seven-fifty on Wednesday morning. And, well—*yawn*—you know, I hate mornings. Of course, it doesn't help that I didn't sleep at all last night. Between my failed dream spell and worrying like crazy all night about Bryce and my friends, there was no sleeping last night. But teaching assistant Cadence Wallace's office hours run eight to nine, and I can't afford to mess up in school this year. Remember Dr. Bainer? Yeah, he still wants to expel me. I think my studies were the other reason Kenosha didn't want me joining their search last night.

I lean back in my comfy black leather chair. Then I take out my cellphone and call Cat on the off chance that she answers . . .

Nope.

This office belongs to my hubby, Professor Bryce Wallace. But it used to belong to my professor and witch mentor, Alondra Johansen. We never changed her furniture. My black leather chair and the fashionable dark mahogany desk with two red suede chairs belonged to my teacher and High Priestess of my coven. We also kept her books. I mean, I have a bunch of her books in our home library, once her home library, but there are many very rare esoteric occultist books on the mahogany shelves here in the office.

I grab one of the books I pulled from a shelf, *The Secret Doctrine,* written by Helena Blavatsky. Do you know Helena Blavatsky? Blavatsky was a Russian occultist of the nineteenth century who founded Theosophy. She believed in some pretty crazy stuff, including that the overseer of our world is not God but a demonic demiurge. Or . . . perhaps more accurately, that there is no God. She believed the fall by the serpent represented the fall of the spirit inside man. She spoke of energy, or shakti, in Kundalini descending from the head to the base of our spine. In other words, the snake, or Lucifer, was a positive force sent down for mankind to bring us into consciousness. Hmm...

Kenosha, Mira, and Bryce never found Cat. Well, as Kenosha said, the woods are over a hundred square miles.

Blavatsky, Blavatsky. Come on, Cadence, remember SCHOOL.

When I first met Alondra, she taught me about the thin veneer separating good from evil in our world. I was a shy young student sitting in one of those red suede chairs across from this desk. And she totally intimidated me that morning. Alondra often used fear and mystery to draw us into witchcraft. She was such a wicked witch. I remember her turning a metal pentagram on this desk, flipping good and evil on its head, just like good 'ole Blavatsky.

There's a knock on the door.

"Mrs. Wallace?" a student asks shyly. The threshold reveals a short girl with shaved dark hair, glasses, and a nose ring, with a backpack slung over her shoulder.

"Have a seat," I say with a smile, pointing to the two red chairs.

"I'm Serena."

"Hey, Serena. What's up?"

But then she clams up and keeps quiet for the longest time. She just sits uncomfortably in the red chair with downcast eyes. So I coax her a little. "Dr. Wallace was covering Galen. Is that what you wanted to discuss?"

She quickly shakes her head.

"Good, I was never very good at ancient Roman history."

She laughs.

"Ancient Egypt?" I ask. "Cleopatra? Or is it something in the Middle Ages we've covered, like the Knights Templar?"

"I want to ask about Dr. Alondra Johansen."

"Well, our teacher was renowned, but she's not in the curriculum," I say with a chuckle. "Did you want to borrow one of her books?"

"Word is that Doctor Johansen was an amazing professor," she says. "She was why I chose this class. I grew up in Hawthorne because Dad works in administration, so coming here was easy enough. I get good grades too. I'm a rare Hawthorne native, my family has lived here all my life, Mrs. Wallace. Then, you know, I came to your husband's class because I love secrets and the occult. But—" Serena puts a hand up. "But I'm not here to talk about class. I need to talk to you about something much more important. And I need you to be totally honest with me."

"I hate secrets, Serena."

Her expression turns sour over that.

"Everyone around college knows what you and your friends do," she says carefully. "It's just that, so many are afraid to come out and say it. Even all the other professors. It's like, they're all afraid because they're afraid of you. But I have to talk about it. I need to talk about what you and your friends do outside of class."

Then she forces her eyes on mine. She seems nervous, but very resolute.

"Serena, this is office hours. Other students are probably waiting in the hallway to discuss class. Whatever you're hearing about outside of lecture is really not important for school." She scowls. So . . . I try another angle. "Why do you want to talk about stuff outside of class?"

For some reason, that does it. She puts her head in her hands and starts crying.

"Are you a witch?" she asks, her voice broken up by tears. "You have to tell me. It could mean life or death."

"Yes. I'm a witch. There are plenty of witches in Wicca."

"That's not what I mean," she snaps. "I'm not referring to Wicca."

"There are also practitioners of Thelema. Even Theosophy, which is what I'll be lecturing on next week, is a popular mystic tradition. Many people are practicing witches these days."

"No, I need to know if you cast *real* magic spells, Mrs. Wallace. The whole school heard about your fight with another witch clan a few years ago. There's no proof, but many people saw it. Some videos were on the internet, but taken down. Gossip says the head witch of another clan named Enora turned into a lion and you hurled her across our field near the library. Then there's another story that you were at church and you fought again with Enora and she transformed into black birds and flew off. All the stories point to you fighting this other witch with *real* magic. Some call you the Hawthorne Witch. But—"

Serena stops. She's rubbing her eyes with the backs of her hands, fighting back tears again. I feel horrible. But I can't say anything. If there's one thing Alondra taught me, it was to keep our craft secret.

"Sorry," she says, taking a deep breath.

"It's okay." I reach into a drawer and hand her some tissue. "It's okay. What's this about?"

"Miley. My sister, Miley, is missing. First, she was sick, then, when morning came, Mom started screaming because her bed was left empty. She disappeared. The only hint about where she went was her window was open. She never sleeps with her window open. And our house opens right into the forest."

"Did you tell the police?"

"My sister was taken by magic, Mrs. Wallace," she snaps disdainfully. "The police can't do anything. There was a witch that hurt her and then kidnapped her. If these are just fake stories about you, then . . . then, God, then there's no hope for my sister. That's why I'm not just talking about your *beliefs* in witchcraft. I'm talking about *real magic*. She was taken by witchcraft. I came to ask for your help with magic, not school."

"How do you know a witch took her?"

"The night of Miley's sickness, a witch had come into Hawthorne Sweets and handed out candy canes. All the candy canes turned into insects, but my sister ate one before the transformation. That was the night of her disappearance. My brother, Colton, claims you were in the restaurant at the time."

Oh, *that* Miley.

"*You were there!*" she insists, opening her eyes wide.

"Serena, these are office hours—"

"God, you have to help us!" she says, jumping up. "Please! You're the Hawthorne Witch. Everyone says you are. I told Mom to talk to you, but she doesn't believe in magic, even though she saw the worms too. You have to help my sister!"

There's a knock on the door. That's the next student, or maybe someone checking to see if we're all right because of Serena's yelling.

"You have no idea where she is?" I ask.

"No," Serena says vehemently, shaking her head. "She's been missing for days. I'm so scared."

"I'll do what I can to help get her back."

Serena searches my eyes.

I walk around the desk and put a hand on her back. She surprises me by jumping into my arms.

"I know you will! I just know it! Please. Please! You don't have to tell me a thing about what you and your friends do, just please help Miley. Please. She's such an angel. I can't believe, of all people, this is happening to her."

Then, before I can say another word, she throws open the door and rushes out.

Behind her is a tall boy with glasses, books tucked under an arm, waiting at the threshold. I know this kid from last year's study group. But my cellphone rings in my pants pocket. It's Bryce.

"Just a moment," I say, raising a finger and forcing a smile.

"Katie, come home," Bryce says. "Everyone's here. We're planning to move out this morning with Ray. And Mira says it shouldn't snow or rain, so it'll be easier to do the search."

"She got Miley, Bryce."

"Who's Miley?"

"That little girl I saw talking to Grýla at Hawthorne Sweets. The one who fell sick. God, that crazy witch kidnapped a little girl! Now it's Cat *and* Miley."

"Well, Raymond's here. So is Kenosha and the whole gang. Everyone is ready to go and search now, but we need our High Priestess. Come home now."

"I'm finishing office hours, babe. There's school too, you know. Kenosha wanted me to cover your office hours—"

"You have to cancel office hours and come home right now, Cadence. Enora's here."

6

GRANULATED SUGAR

"Oh, hi Katie." Enora greets me at my front door in a scarlet cloak with her black lace collar. "How are you?"

"What the hell are you doing here, Enora?"

It's not only my archenemy; my whole entryway is full of her scarlet-cloaked goons from her Abaddon coven. Cordelia, Enora's lackey, is stupidly pretending to be offended by my attitude, as usual. You remember that huge bitch. You know, the one with black tattoos covering her face who hung Beatrix a couple years ago in my outdoor patio?

Bryce and Maddie, wearing black robes, rush toward them.

"Katie," Bryce says, "Katie, I let 'em in. Hear them out before you throw them out."

"Well, Cadence," Enora says with her infernal smirk, "seems another maga's decided to attack us from Hawthorne? And it seems, as usual, you don't know what the hell is going on. Well, I'm here to help. I'm always ready for a fight."

"For the last time, I'm not fighting you, Enora."

"I said I'm here to help, Cadence, not fight."

"Everything's prepared outside, High Priestess," Maddie says, out of breath. She hands me a spare black robe. "Willow and Raven have organized the bonfire. Everyone's ready for the meeting."

"You want the Abaddon coven in our backyard, Maddie?" I ask.

"I invited them, Cadence," Bryce replies. "I think Cat needs all the help she can get."

"Yes," Enora replies. "Yes, and we have accepted your Oungan's invitation. But do we have yours, Windstorm?"

"She's never been very respectful, Master." Cordelia is looking down at me with a big smirk.

"You're the one who isn't respectful!" God, as much as I can't stand Enora, I hate Cordelia even more. "All of you villains are outlaws with the council. And most of you belong in prison."

"But if we're going to find our sister Brittany," Enora says solemnly, "seems we need to put our differences aside and work together again."

"Brittany was taken from us in your forest," says a short, quiet witch in a red robe. This witch is a half-shaven blond, like Cat was last year, but with black tattoos—mainly numbers—covering the bald side and her cheek and neck. She looks even younger than Cat. "We're all hurting from this witch, Windstorm."

"Brittany was one of their newest recruits," Bryce explains. "Their youngest. She was only sixteen. Whatever's going on, it's attacking Enora's coven. The search isn't only for Cat and Miley now, it's for their witch too."

"Dream casting is one thing," Enora says. "Kidnapping is quite another. As much as we have our differences, I know you'd never stoop so low as to kidnap one of my sisters, Cadence. This isn't a fight with you."

"Can they join us this morning, Cadence?" Bryce asks.

"Whatever," I say, throwing up my hands.

I make my way around all the red-cloaked bodies and head to our living room. Unfortunately, Enora and her red-robed goons trail me down the main hallway.

"You're showing well," Enora quips, standing behind me. "By the way, I was scrying when you had that blue dream. What a lovely *ville*. I thought the blue was very Kenneth Anger. But the best part was when you were making out with that really handsome man."

I whirl around. The bitch is stupidly smirking.

"Who do you think conjured the cat, Cadence?" she asks. "Might just resolve all the mystery. It wasn't me."

"You can join our meeting, Enora," I say, raising my brow, "but if you get out of line, you and your witches are out of my house. Okay?"

"Sure, Katie," Enora says with a stupid grin. "Sure thing."

My backyard is packed with black cloaks surrounding our central bonfire. White plastic chairs surround the fire, on the wild grass and patches of snow circled by Hawthorne Forest. My coven brought twice as many chairs as usual to accommodate all twelve of our archenemy scarlet-cloaked "friends." None of my black-robed witches look happy to see them. And the bonfire seems super weird under a clear morning sky and bright sun. We never hold ceremony during the day.

Kenosha's already seated. She's wigless, not looking like our dean, but like a forest witch in her green cloak and all these gold necklaces and bracelets. Sitting beside her are Beth, Noori, Abella, Debra, Courtney, Josie, and all the other witches in my coven. Maddie and Bryce approach three open chairs. But then—

"Cadence?"

It's Raymond. Wearing suspenders, he's the only one who looks "normal." The poor guy's eyes are bloodshot.

"I'm so sorry, Raymond," I say, embracing him. "I'm sorry."

"You mind if I join your search?"

I shake my head with a rueful grin, touching his shoulder. He sits down quietly on the opposite side of the fire, near the scarlet-robed witches.

My antebellum house stands behind me. And the forest surrounds us, calming me. All these trees circling the wild grass glade are like a large mother's arms, like blessed Hecate, coming down in one large embrace.

"*Yatu*," I say. I stand and lift my arms before the flames. Quickly, I recite the formal words of ceremony: "Blessed be the day that the circle is brought together. Blessed be the coven under our gods Gaia, Selene, and Astraeus. *Lux alba et tenebris. Atman.*" There, formality's over. "Guys—"

"Glory be the morning star," Enora utters stupidly across from me. Her witches snicker.

"Let's dispense with the formalities, shall we?" Enora asks. "We're meeting with your coven to discuss how we're going to—"

"Cadence is officiating, Enora," Bryce interjects beside me.

"It's okay, Bryce," I object, sitting back down. "It's fine. She's right. I was just about to say we don't have much time."

"Brittany," Enora continues, "was heading back home to meet with us in Atlanta. She and her boyfriend stopped to get gas in your little town. The imbecile said he lost her when he went to pay. He thinks she wandered into your forest. Well, she had a phone. The phone texted me an hour later with the words *'growly, growler.'* Sound familiar? I happen to remember scrying those exact words—"

"You were spying on us again, Enora?" snaps Maddie.

"Hey, don't blame me," Enora says, touching her chest. "Your fake dean is hell bent on arresting me."

"Sooner or later, you'll be imprisoned," Kenosha says. "If it weren't for your lost friend, I would have already called the police."

"Sure, Willow," Enora says, "sure. Anyway, last night, Cadence, you tried your hand at some of my illegal black magic yourself. You used necromancy to scry a cat. Right? And you had that lovely blue dream."

"Keep my business, my business," I warn her, raising my eyebrows.

I glance at Bryce. I haven't told him about my weird dream yet.

"But you summoned a cat, right?" Enora asks. "Just not the daughter of our guest. You summoned a demon cat. What does that tell you? This enemy is attacking you. The witch cast magic in your sleep on your hallowed ground."

"But I'm not sure I was attacked. I'm not as good at divination as you. It could have just been a dream or a botched spell."

"I felt two energies with us last night," Enora says, lifting two fingers. "Two. There was more than just you there. And you don't botch spells. No, there's a new power invading the ether surrounding Hawthorne. Samhain's been pleasantly quiet since we took care of her."

"Katie took care of her," corrects Bryce.

"Sure," continues Enora. "I heard you witnessed a transmutation of candy, Cadence? Apparently, this sick hag likes to tempt kids. Well, guess what? Brittany was our youngest initiate. She's the youngest initiate I've ever let join my coven."

"Beatrix was your youngest witch," snaps Courtney, real pissed. And Courtney, one of the nicest people I've ever known, looks ready to clobber her. Because Beatrix was killed by Enora's coven, and Beatrix was

Courtney's best friend. "I don't think we should let them join us in our search today, Cadence."

"I second that," Mira says.

Enora turns to Raymond, by her side. "How old is your daughter, ghost hunter?"

"Seventeen," says Raymond.

"Twisted bitch is going after kids," Enora says with a shrug. "Look, Courtney, I mustn't be so bad. You would never have married your lover if it weren't for me."

"Shut up, Panthera," snaps Courtney. "*You—*"

"Calm the hell down," Enora says. "Whatever, all right? We're here to help Hawthorne fight this witch. We have to work together. The witch is attacking both our covens."

"Sit down, guys," I say. "Come on." I'm trying to look calm, but honestly I don't totally disagree with Courtney.

"The Abaddon coven shouldn't be here, High Priestess," Courtney repeats.

"We have to help the kids." I turn to Kenosha. "Kenosha, Melanie told Maddie and me that the energy around this season feeds off the young. That might be some hint as to why the children are being abducted."

"This time of the Beldani wheel is one of death," Kenosha says. She turns to my coven's new recruits. "Yule, or Christmas, comes after celebrating the death of the witches' new year in October, Samhain. It's this time of year when everything freezes and dies and the circle is up for renewal. If stuck, the wheel becomes unbalanced, tilting towards lifelessness, and seeks the energy of our youth. This explains the Christmas tale of Grýla in Iceland. Many think Grýla is a myth to explain the deaths of children lost in the snow covered forest. Or, similarly, there's the other Christmas monster, Krampus, that punishes naughty children who stray from their parents' rules and protection. All these myths center around dark energy overpowering the light of the young and innocent during the harsh winter. The greatest power of the sun comes from our young. In fact, some more sinister, dark practitioners try to harness this energy from children."

"Grýla seems to be feeding off this season's energy," I say.

"What does this have to do with Grýla, Cadence?" asks Enora. "Willow just said she's a myth."

"Grýla is the witch who attacked Miley in our ice cream parlor. She called herself Grýla."

"And who the hell's Miley?" Enora snaps. "Cadence, if you want me and my witches to help, you're gonna have to tell me and my coven everything."

"We don't want your help," says Mira.

"Miley is the little girl that's missing with Cat," I say. "She got sick when Grýla turned the candy canes to worms."

"Can you scry this witch, Master?" asks Cordelia.

"I can scry anyone, Adder," replies Enora. "But I can't very well scry a witch I've never seen. Tell me, what does this Grýla look like? Do you have anything of hers? Clothes? Keepsakes? Leftover food? Those candies that turned to worms? Give me an object and I can find her through my black mirror."

"She looks like Mother Shipton," Bryce says. "She's a classic hunched-over old witch in tattered clothes with a long nose and warts. We've seen her rummaging through trash on campus. She's homeless, which fits the Grýla legend. Grýla used to snatch children while she was dressed like a beggar."

"A woman rummaging through trash at Hawthorne University," Enora says, bursting out laughing, "has kidnapped two witches from our covens? A bum kidnapped Brittany? Come on! You have to be kidding. You guys have this all wrong."

"The woman is possessed by a demon," Kenosha says earnestly.

"You fucking think everybody's possessed by a demon," says Enora. "Look, just show me the bitch and then my witches and I will kill her. Possessed or not. Simple and easy. Right, witches?"

"Yes, Master," say many witches in red, nodding their heads.

"You can't kill her, stupid," Mira says, rolling her eyes. "If it's a possession, the Ekimmu will simply move to another vessel. We need to go after the source."

"Who listens to you, Raven?" asks Enora.

"You're lucky Windstorm is allowing you here in her backyard," Kenosha replies. "I should have called the police."

"Go ahead. Maybe we can waste time casting curses instead of finding our lost kids?"

"You have no business scrying anyone," says Kenosha.

Chandra kicks me. Is she getting riled up by the fight? I hardly blame you, sweetheart. There are few people more irritating than Enora. But I'm kicked again. No . . . it's something else. *What? What is it, Chandra?*

There's a taste of granulated sugar along my lips. I lick my lips again. It tastes so sweet and yummy. It's like someone poured a whole jar of sugar over them. And . . . there's a creamy taste too. Like a wonderful swirl of thick rich chocolate ganache.

Of course, Kenosha, Mira, Courtney, Maddie, Cordelia, and Enora are now standing and screaming at each other, ready to clobber one another. That's no surprise. The surprise is that they didn't go at it the minute we walked outside.

"Shut up, guys, 'kay?" I say. "Shut up for a second." I stand up and start scanning the trees. "Grýla's casting. Chandra always kicks when I taste sugar."

"But it's your hallowed ground, Cadence," says Maddie, sitting under me, sounding creeped out. "*Stop fighting and shut up, guys!*" Maddie cries. "*Katie's sensing the witch is here right now!*"

That quiets them. Enora pulls out her long thin black wand and searches the woods too. Then Mira, Bryce, and Kenosha search the trees.

"Call your watchers, Cadence," Kenosha suggests, looking everywhere. "Ask them to find her. The witch will lead us to the kids."

I hear cackling. It's a witch's laughter mixed with the sound of babies crying.

"*Coward!*" cries Enora, jumping up. "*Take one of mine? Wait till I get my hands on you!*"

But then everything falls quiet. Too quiet . . .

A wind gently brushes through the wild grass as clouds rush overhead at unnatural speed, at times blocking the sun. Then a few leaves flutter, and some small branches sway. The wind blows harder and trees sway. That's followed by a tempest so strong that it sways some of the tree trunks. Bryce leaps up and holds me just in time before I'm thrown to the ground. Many other witches are knocked down. It's such a powerful gale that it douses our large bonfire. But then . . .

Silence again. It's like, just another clear-skied sunny day.

"Was that one of you?" Enora asks, totally spooked. "Cadence?"

I shake my head, searching the trees.

"I think this witch has more power than just transforming candy, guys," Mira says, standing back up, with her eyes bulging.

I see a shadow running under a tree a few yards away. Is it her? It's too dark to tell. But I think I see white eyes.

"Goetia!" I cry. *"Goetia, Goetia, Goetia!"*

My casting is partly a reflex to get Grýla—or whoever it is—out from hiding in the woods. The other part is to follow Kenosha's advice and bring out the dark shadows I control.

Tall dark shades fly from their hiding places in tree branches and behind tree trunks. Darkness occludes the sun above. My friends can't see the demons, but they see a shadow engulfing my glade. And it turns so cold.

Shadows converge over a figure hiding in the trees. I hear wailing. Then the dark figure is consumed in a black, spinning tornado. And she's gone.

And it's quiet again.

"Lux!" I cry, raising my arms. The bonfire relights. And the sun shines brightly through clouds above.

"Nativitatis Maga. Catrina. Show me Catrina! By Hecate, show Cat, Miley, and Brittany's location to the Hawthorne Witch! Reveal yourself to the Hawthorne and Abaddon covens now."

But the cackling returns, echoing more loudly in the forest.

"Bitch!" Enora cries, swinging her thin wand in the direction of laughter. She strikes her wand against a black book she's clutching at her chest shouting, *"Manifesta Amica! Resurgo. Resurgo. Upon Hawthorne, corvus. Resurgo. Yule Maga! Show yourself! And bring back Brittany! Corvus, corvus, corvus!"*

A rush of caws thunders from the branches of the trees. And then hundreds of black birds swarm out—so many birds fly up into the sky that the sun's rays are blocked out again.

"Between your magic and mine, we'll find her, Windstorm!" Enora cries. *"Come on Abaddon witches. Let's get her!"*

And Enora runs with her red-cloaked witches into the trees.

"Wait, Enora!" I cry. "Wait! Stay here in my backyard with us!"

The sugary taste has left my lips. And Chandra's calming down inside my belly. I think the witch is gone.

"We have to plan this out, guys!" I shout. *"Stop, Enora! Stop! Stop running away!"*

But Enora and her whole red-robed group disappear into a dark fog in the trees. Many of my sisters from my circle—Abella, Josie, Nancy, Beth, and Noori—aren't far behind them. That's followed by cawing and a rush of more ravens.

"Wait! Stop, guys!"

7

GIANT GREEN GUMDROP

Snowflakes slowly float down, landing as white fluff on tree branches, leaves, and our muddy path as I'm walking beside Bryce under a thick forest canopy. It's beautiful when yellow rays of sunlight occasionally break through tree branches. But although it's nearly midday, the fog is thick enough to make it as dark as night. Ever since I summoned demons, it seems darkness has fallen everywhere. My hands are digging in my jeans pockets under my cloak, and Bryce is holding me tightly. Meanwhile our witchy flat black boots keep crunching on ice mixed with leaves and pine needles. But despite all the cold, I still smell that scent of elm and earthy wet mud from the forest I love.

Bryce helps me over a large fallen tree trunk. I have to hand him my old leather-bound grimoire, *Broomstick*, for a second as I lean on my arms, hands in knitted gray gloves pressed against the hard, spiky bark. Then we're back to meandering down the dirt path, covered with patches of snow.

I hear shouting. It's Enora's shrill voice. How can someone so pretty have such an annoying voice? She's so loud, but she's probably miles from here. We've lost her and the others. But I still see her birds. Ravens are everywhere, perched on branches, on ice, or along the muddy path. Some of their small shadows are sweeping from branch to branch above.

And yet, aside from blackbird wings fluttering, and Enora barking, it's pretty quiet.

"Do insects freeze when it's icy cold out, Bryce?" I ask. "I always wondered why it seems quieter when it snows."

"Bugs die in the cold, Kate. They just lay eggs."

"Oh, that'd be why," I say with a nod, squeezing him close. "You're so smart."

"I'm your professor. Look, it's been hours and you're getting cold. I'm worried about Cat, but we have to head back soon. Maybe regroup for another search with the others tomorrow?"

"Where'd they all go? It's weird. I thought Maddie and Mira were right behind us?"

"I keep hearing their voices. They haven't strayed that far off."

"Do you even know how to get back?"

"Yes . . ." He stops walking and looks around. "I think so. We've circled a few times. We're not too far from our house."

"Bryce, Cat won't survive another night alone. We have to keep searching. We just have to."

There's another break in the clouds and, for a moment, the entire forest brightens enough for me to have to squint and avert my eyes.

And then I hear whispers.

"Did you hear that?"

He nods. But he doesn't look like he wanted to.

I lift a tree branch from the snow, blow at some moss and leaves at the tip with my frosty breath, and mutter "*lux.*" Then the branch is aflame.

"At least I'm with a powerful witch," Bryce quips.

It's then, under firelight from my makeshift torch, that I find something lying by my black boots on the snowy trail. I kneel for a better look. It's so weird. It's a piece of brown crust with a white center lying in the snow. I try to pick it up, but it's hard to grab anything in these thick snow gloves. Bryce reaches down to help with his bare hands—but then we lurch back when one of Enora's ravens swoops down and snatches it from his hand.

"Shoo!" I say. "Shoo! Go away! Get out of here! God, her stupid birds are everywhere, Bryce! They're as annoying as she is."

"What was that?" Bryce says, staring at our find. "A breadcrumb? Are we supposed to be Hansel and Gretel? Is this witch playing a bad joke?"

I spot another breadcrumb a few yards farther down the path and point at it.

"So, you're Gretel and I'm Hansel, Cadence? I really don't like this. This witch might be nuttier than Melanie."

"Wouldn't know with all of Enora's stupid birds. I think the woods have turned darker with her birds and my spellcasting."

Whispers interrupt our talking again. So this time, I whisper back.

"*Nativitatis Maga. Nativitatis Maga.* By Hecate, reveal yourself to Hawthorne, Yuletide Witch."

"*Cadence! Cadence!*"

Bryce and I spin around in the direction of the shouting. That was Cat's voice! I'm forced to squint as the sun's rays open again through a gap in the trees. But then Cat stops crying for help.

Light shines over our dirt path, winding through the trees, and I see more breadcrumbs strewn along the ground. I don't follow the path. Instead, I walk off the trail and start gathering large fallen branches in the bushes. I pile the thickest ones and start forming a five-pointed star.

"What are you doing, Katie?" Bryce asks.

"I don't know. I remember doing this in my dream. All this happened before, in the dream...or...I foresaw it happening. You and I first spotted breadcrumbs. So I built this sigil as a signal and as a refuge during the nightmare. I think the headmaster's right, this witch is very powerful. She, or whoever's possessing her, is attacking us with powerful magic. I feel like I have to build this circle for protection."

And I drag another stick along the ice, forming a circle surrounding my pentagram. Then I gesture at my work.

Bryce nods, but then he freaks me out when he covers his eyes, squinting over my left shoulder. Turning in the direction of his gaze, I see a bright golden glow. The light is heralding a small cottage among the trees. The breadcrumb trail ends at a walkway surrounding the cottage, which has two windows with shutters and a chimney. It's as if the cottage has always been there, hidden in the woods. Two large red poles with white stripes by the entrance appear to be the size of people. They look like huge peppermint candy canes. And beside the peppermint sticks, in the snow, are two gingerbread-like statues about half my height. The top of one of the peppermint sticks forms the outline of a girl's face. But her expression is frozen, motionless, like a statue. An icy pathway of shiny red and green candy tiles leads to the front door. The door and the shutters are composed of a brown cake-like substance. Gingerbread? White patches on the walls form a thick plaster. On the plaster brush marks stick out in sections, reminding me of frosting. Soft red and green gems embedded in the white plaster, covered in crystalized sugar kernels, reflect the golden sunlight. Gumdrops or sugar plums. Chocolatey-brown drippings fall from the rooftops, draining into chocolate pools. And the roof is made of a cinnamon red candy–like surface.

We walk slowly along the candy path. Bryce runs a finger along the white plaster beside the door. It's not solid, and it's not plaster, it's like a thick white goo.

"Frosting?" Bryce asks me with a nervous chuckle.

I nod and run my finger along the wall too. I bring the goo to my nose. It smells so sweet and delicious.

"This has to stop," snaps Bryce. "This sick witch is controlling us like in a fairy tale. And . . . I feel drowsy, as if I'm dreaming, Kate. I think she's putting a spell on us."

How can she not be? We're standing in front of a gingerbread house.

I nab a large crystalized green gumdrop the size of my palm, stuck to the white frosting, and bite into it. It tastes so good! It's soft, full of granules of sugar, with a wonderful tangy sweet lime. And the best part is the consistency. The gob sticks in my mouth like chewing gum.

"Cadence, what are you doing!"

He tries to snatch it from my fingers, but I pull it away. I don't know why I'm eating it, but I am. It's like I'm compelled to eat it. But it tastes sooo good. I don't know how Bryce is stopping himself. I'm so hungry.

"It tastes really good, Bryce," I say with my mouth full. "Wow. You should try some." Then I dip it in some of the wall plaster and offer him some. "Try it, babe. Just take a bite."

"Growly, growler. Growly, growler."

That stops my chomping.

"Cadence, what's going on?"

"Try your phone, Bryce. Try to call the others."

But I lick the uneaten edge of my giant gumdrop. Those crystals seem to pop on my tongue.

"See . . . see if you can reach Kenosha or Mira, Bryce."

But as he reaches for his phone, he touches a red gumdrop fixed to the wall. This one's smaller, about the size of his fingertip. He puts his cellphone back in his pocket and throws the gumdrop in his mouth. All the while, I'm still busy dipping my gumdrop in the frosting, swirling it around to get just the right amount of frosting dip, and then taking more bites out of it. Bryce runs his hand along the soft, sweet glaze covering the wall and starts licking his fingers. Then he bites down on some of my gumdrop.

"Open the door, Bryce," I say, with my mouth still full. "Come on, we have to help the kids."

When he's hesitant, I open the door.

The cottage is made up of only three large rooms. One side, to my right, is the kitchen, another a dining room, and another is some sort of storage room full of large wooden crates. A wooden table spans most of the central room with food piled up over an elegant white tablecloth. Cakes, cupcakes, éclairs, donuts, tiramisu, ice cream dishes, cookies, macaroons, brownies, mixed berry parfait, raspberry, powdered sugar, snickerdoodle cookies, chocolate mousse, pina colada lasagna, chocolate soufflé, and some yummy treats that are covered in chocolate and vanilla swirled frosting.

"Growly, growler. Growly, Growler."

In the kitchen, the mad witch is mumbling those words to herself, crouched over a fiery stove and large black cauldron. The old hag's still wearing the same tatters as in the ice cream parlor—a worn brown cloth dress with a black hood covering her head. She's hunched over, with her back to us, turning a huge wooden spoon in a boiling brew in the cauldron. The cauldron is a couple feet wide.

I hear children crying. But it seems to be coming from inside the walls.

Then I lurch back and gasp as a child's drenched head emerges from Grýla's huge cauldron. A dark-haired boy climbs out of the huge pot with a dripping T-shirt and shorts, as if emerging from a relaxing dip in a Jacuzzi. He walks over to the other side of the cottage, where I saw the stacked boxes. Then the wet boy opens a box and crawls in. He closes a wooden door on himself.

Wait . . . those aren't crates at the opposite side of the house—they're wooden cages. Inside all the cages are children! *And I see Cat!* She's packed like a sardine in one of the small wooden cages with her arms folded around her legs. It seems she can barely fit. I'm not sure why she doesn't just kick the door open. I don't see a lock. Instead of fighting, Cat keeps closing her eyes and sucking on a straw. Some chocolatey goo has fallen all over her neck and stained her white T-shirt.

"Come in, Pappa, come in," Grýla says, stirring her pot, cocking her head back. "Try some treats. Let's see, we have so many treats for children to eats. And for Pappa too. Yes we do, yes we do."

"*Run, Cadence!*" shouts Cat, suddenly opening her eyes wide. "*Run! Get out of here while you can!*"

Grýla whirls around at Cat and shouts, "*Make 'em plump, make 'em strong! So they may run, run, run along!*"

I feel possessed by terrible hunger. I rush to the table and start shuffling éclairs in my mouth. I grab a blueberry parfait. Some of the jelly drips down my lips. I bite into a chocolate donut, dipping it in the chocolate mousse. I smear it all by running the back of my hand over my lips.

"*Leave her alone!*" screams Cat. "*Cadence! No! God, stop her! Please stop her!*"

Grýla bursts into laughter.

Then I hear something scurry behind me. Running by the wall is a large black cat. The black cat bends down, bubbles, and distorts, and then forms into a huge broad-shouldered, dark-skinned man. He is naked. I recognize him as that oaf in my blue dream. His eyes shimmer sapphire. And he's nearly twice the height of Bryce.

"Go, Bryce," I say weakly, gathering a handful of sugar-coated raisins. "Run to the protective circle I made outside."

"Leave?" asks Grýla. "But why? Pappa, why would you leave while the stew's hot? I brew such a nice broth for you two. Mamma and Pappa are my guests. First, try a candy snack before you go. Go ahead. Eat for Chandra. It tastes so sweet and gobbly."

Grýla points to bright red hard candy in a small barrel by the door.

Bryce runs to the door. I'm thinking he's rushing out to get to my circle, but no—he lands on his knees and starts funneling the red candy into his mouth.

"Eat, eat!" storms Grýla, laughing. She hobbles to me. "More and more! Let's see . . . in my pockets, why, what else do I have here for you, child?" She digs in the pockets of her tattered dress. Then she pulls out some things wrapped in plastic. "See, I have fingers and toes, dear. Fingers and toes!"

Inside the plastic, I see fingers and a bloody, torn fingernail.

"Get out, Bryce!" I shout with my mouth full. "Run to my protective circle!"

But Bryce is too weak.

I feel really weak too. And...sleepy. This witch is casting a spell on us. Last time a witch made me feel this tired, it was Enora fighting me in her lair.

That cat-man grabs Bryce in his huge arms. With one hand, he tears Bryce's shirt off, then he raises Bryce's arms, chaining each wrist to the wall.

"Jola, hand me my athame," Grýla says. "Just more of a taste will pleasure them well enough."

The cat-man hands her a small dagger. Grýla runs dirty fingers with long fingernails along the black handle. Then she runs the silver tip along Bryce's muscular chest and stomach, drawing a line of blood.

"*No!*" I shout. "*You stay away from him!*"

"Handsome, handsome pappa," she remarks.

"*You stay away from him!*" I shout. I raise my grimoire, *Broomstick*, aloft before the witch. "Show your true self. I command you. This is my hallowed ground! *Vade retro demon! Vade retro!* Demon, leave this woman! Leave this vessel!"

The large cat-man disappears. The cabin fades. And for a moment, Grýla looks everywhere around her, disoriented. She puts her head in her hands and shakes it.

But then the house reappears as quickly as it vanished.

"*You have no power here!*" I shout. "*Leave this vessel! I command you, demon. Ekimmu, leave this vessel! The Hawthorne Witch commands you to leave!*"

"*Stop her, Cadence!*" cries Cat.

Grýla licks the blood from the tip of her knife. Then she runs the bloody knife along Bryce's chest again, smearing it red while cackling.

"I'd stop your laughing!" I shout. "There's an army of witches outside searching for the kids. How are you going to defend against all of them?"

"Aren't you pregnant, dear?" the witch asks, turning to me. Her eyes have turned pearly white. "Feed your baby, feed me. Hungry? Don't worry, your lips be free. Have some more for Chandra. Go ahead. Anything your heart desires in my home. After, when full, the sweetest treat awaits from my pot. Welcome home, child. *My* home be my hallowed ground. Might be your forest, but this be *my* home."

I struggle to keep my eyes open. Bryce's eyes are closed.

Everything blurs. That huge cat-man is back to being a large black cat. It's a Bombay cat, now just brushing his furry back against Bryce's legs.

"And after you have your fill," Grýla says, "sit in the cage by your friend. I have one made for Chandra. Relinquish your book and sit in the cage for your baby. And then . . . guess what? Guess what treat I have for you and your child?"

She takes the book from my hands and I swoon, having difficulty standing.

"What?" I mutter.

"*Milkshakes! Milkshakes!*"

Then the witch guffaws again.

"Now open," Grýla commands. "Open." I lurch back when her wrinkled face and long, crooked nose are right up against my face. Her breath is foul. "Go ahead."

My mouth opens without my control. Grýla throws a handful of orange, green and blue gumballs in my mouth. I chew through the hard shells and the soft centers. It's the sweetest bubble gum I've ever tasted. Then I breathe in a wonderful smell of cinnamon, nutmeg, chocolate, and sugar. And that cornucopia of food on the huge wooden table is under me.

"*Eat, eat,*" she mutters with a nod. "*Navitas Nativitatis. Navitas Nativitatis.* Do you have any idea what I will get out of the sacrifice of you and your unborn child?"

I get on my knees before the table.

"That's it," Grýla cries, bursting into laughter. "*Navitas Nativitatis.* That's it. Eat, drink. Eat to your heart's content. Then vomit it all up. Throw it all up. Then eat more. Upon Saturnalia, eat and eat. And then have more and more and more. *More and more and more!*"

With my teeth, I pick up two large nutty almond brownies with thick fudge frosting. Crumbling it, smearing the chocolate all over my nose and cheeks, I take it all into my mouth. As I swirl the chocolate and run my tongue along my lips and cheeks, I hear crying. Cat's weeping.

Another head bobs up from the water in Grýla's pot. It's Miley! Her long blond hair is drenched. But she doesn't appear to be in pain. She seems to be in a trance, soaking in a gentle pool or sauna.

I dig my face back into the brownies.

"Growly, Growler. Growly, Growler."

8

COTTON CANDY

IN A SCARLET HAZE, I FOLLOW A WINDING PATH THROUGH A DARK, ROCKY cave. A pleasant breeze blows along my cheeks carrying sugary whiffs of strawberry and cherry. After I turn a corner, the haze turns dark violet and the smell changes to blueberry. And yet there's a hint of a lovelier sweetness. It's from a stairway cut into the stone painted a slick nutty brown, as if made of chocolate. I'm holding a single dim black candle. And under my rotund stomach, my tanned bare feet look so dark as my toes pass over white flour. It's cold. I shiver. I bring the candle up to my lips to blow it out. Then I take a bite out of the hot candle stalk. It tastes like hot, melting black licorice. And as I slowly meander over white flour, it feels cold as ice, but as white and fluffy as cotton candy.

9

SCRYING FOR WITCHES

"The sun's dropping, it's cold, and we're getting nowhere fast," Enora grumbles, cocking her head back at Maddie and Mira while clutching her arms tightly around her scarlet cloak. "We've been walking for hours."

"And you're complaining as usual," Mira mutters under her breath, rolling her eyes. She's walking behind Enora with Maddie.

"*Revelare*," Enora cries. "*Revelare*. Reveal yourself, witch! Where the hell are you! How long do we have to search this forest for you, coward?"

"Katie could have planned our search if you hadn't run off," Maddie says.

Mira halts. Then she crouches by a tree, closes her eyes, and cups her hand, scooping some soft dirt under the trunk. Here, under the canopy, this is one of the only dry spots. A raven swoops and lands on her shoulder, and she opens her eyes, annoyed, brushing it off. She sniffs the dirt on her palm, letting the sand kernels drift between her fingers.

"We need to find the girls before sunset," Mira says, standing up. "It would be nice if you called off your stupid birds, Enora. As usual, you're fighting against everyone and everything."

Enora's cellphone rings under her red cloak. She reaches into a pocket in her pants.

"Yeah?" Enora says, cradling her phone over her shoulder.

"Thought you didn't believe in using phones?" Maddie quips.

Enora shows Maddie her middle finger.

"Cordelia, where are you?" Enora asks. "Huh? Well, you'll never guess who's with me right now."

Mira surveys the woods. Then she crouches down and steadies her breath, closing her eyes again.

"Bryce and Cadence are still missing," Maddie says almost in a whisper, crouching beside her. "I called but she won't answer her phone. Why? Is it all these clouds and fog mucking up the reception? It's never stopped the signal before. I've never not been able to reach her out here."

"Breadcrumbs?" Enora asks in her phone, laughing. "Breadcrumbs? What the hell are you saying, Adder?" She stupidly laughs harder than ever. "What are you smoking? You're seeing breadcrumbs in the snow? Either you've gone looney or it's our Christmas witch."

"Anything, Meer?" Maddie whispers, laying a hand on her back.

"No, Maddie," Mira says, shaking her head. "Afraid not."

Enora stuffs her phone back in her pocket.

"They've found nothing," Enora says. "Nothing but a stupid trail of breadcrumbs. Twisted Christmas-bitch thinks we're in a goddamn fairy tale. Wait till I meet her and she tries offering me candy."

"Wait, Maddie, look over there!" Mira says. She's pointing to a bunch of sticks on the ground in a small snowy clearing among the trees. "This looks fresh."

"Mira? Madison?" cries Kenosha's voice.

Kenosha emerges from between two trees in her long forest green robe. Following her is a large group of black robes and Raymond.

"*Yatu*, Raven," Kenosha says, approaching. "Have you found Cadence?"

"Look," Mira says, still staring down. "It's fresh, Willow. But I'm not sure why it's here."

"Didn't Cadence say she made a pentacle, in her dream, to protect her a couple days ago?" asks Kenosha, staring at the find. "Maybe she built a real one to let us know where she is."

"Come on," Enora says, "you guys probably make symbols here all the time."

"Why would High Priestess make a pentagram, Doctor Trent?" asks Beth. Our other new recruits, Nancy and Noori, look over too.

"It's a pentacle, Beth," corrects Kenosha. "A pentacle is a pentagram in a circle. See the circle in the snow around it? Both the pentagram and pentacle are powerful sigils. They can be used for protection. Remember what your daughter, Cat, asked during the séance, Raymond? She asked if we should run a circle of salt around our séance table. Well, during ceremony, sometimes we chalk a circle around our bonfire. This small circle is an area of protection. The pentacle was first used by Babylonians to cast apotropaic spells. Like a lucky charm or a cross warding off a vampire."

"You think Cadence formed this for protection?" Maddie asks.

"Or as a beacon," Kenosha suggests. "And you, felon?" asks Kenosha, turning to Enora. "Have your sisters found anything?"

"Just breadcrumbs," Enora replies with a smirk.

"I'm getting really worried about Cadence," Maddie says. "She's still missing, Kenosha."

Then Maddie turns and looks right at me.

I'm right here, Maddie! Don't you see me? Right here!

All the other witches lean over the snow, studying my symbol on the ground. But Maddie is still staring in my direction.

She furrows her brow. Then her eyes open wide.

"She's here, guys," Maddie says. She tugs at Mira's arm and points in my direction. "Cadence is right there."

You can see me?

"How do you know, Maddie?" asks Mira. "I don't see a thing."

"I see her," Maddie replies, staring. "I mean . . . I don't see her . . . I sense her. Or I feel her, I think."

"You're staring at trees," Enora quips.

I can't seem to show the rest of them. I don't even know how Maddie's seeing me. We've all thought my best friend has empathic powers.

My knees throb. I'm bent like a pretzel so tightly in this small wooden cage. There's a long straw around my neck running past my cheek. It's full of this really yummy peppermint stick, caramel, and chocolate shake, and I keep feeling compelled to suck it. My heart's racing. And I have a constant ache of hunger.

If I could make enough noise, maybe more of my friends would hear? Or perhaps I could directly talk to Maddie through magical telepathy?

Cat's trapped beside me. She's been whimpering. There are no locks. It's this horrible witch's magic keeping us caged. Cat's face is so messy from spilling that same nasty, wonderful-tasting stuff from a plastic straw. Other kids are in traps below us. They're drinking the chocolate shake poison too.

I stare forward using all my magical intent to see through the wall again. But then I'm too distracted by what's chained before me. Bryce. His eyes are closed, but he keeps wincing in pain. Blood still covers his chest where he was cut by that dagger, but it's dried. And running along his legs is that black demon cat.

I jump. Grýla appears crouched down beside me, opening one of the cages. She yanks out a little blond-haired girl. Miley! The poor little girl is screaming.

"*No! No!*"

"Back in the pot, little one," Grýla says. "Come on. Back inside. Come, come. Back in the water. With all your friends outside, I need you to take a dip for just another small, sweet taste of your lovely baby skin. Or, maybe, maybe, just maybe...*a little more?*" She laughs. "Maybe...a finger or a toe?"

"*Leave her alone!*" screams Cat. "My God! Cadence! Cadence, open your eyes! She's going to hurt Miley!"

"*Shut up!*" Grýla says. "If I hear any more crying from you, I'll do more than use her as stock for my soup, I'll serve you as my main course! You whine too much. You're naughtier than the rest. Even more than this sweet, sweet baby child." Grýla smiles down at Miley. "Now come on, my little sweetness. Back in the pot for another lovely dip."

"No!" Miley says, crying. "*I won't! I won't! Leave me alone!*"

Cat kicks her trap open. She charges at Grýla and tugs at Miley's arm.

"*Let her go!*"

"*Let go of me or I'll baste you!*"

"*Let her go!*" Cat screams. "*Let her go!*" Then she turns to me. "*Cadence! Cadence! Open your eyes. You have to help us!*"

I didn't realize my eyes were shut.

"*Stop it!*" cries Miley. "*Stop! Please, please just leave me alone!*"

The little girl's cries are enough to jar me awake.

"She's in trouble," Maddie says.

For a flash, I see all the witches staring in my direction, seeming to finally notice me. And now more scarlet robes are arriving in the woods just in time. There must be thirty witches surrounding Grýla's cottage.

"She's in that weird gingerbread house," Maddie says, pointing again.

"Gingerbread house?" Enora asks scornfully.

"Where do you see her, Maddie?" asks Kenosha.

"Maddie," I say in a forceful whisper. "Maddie, Grýla's going to hurt Miley! You're right, I'm right in front of you. You all have to help us. Quick! You have to go through the front door of the house now!"

But Maddie squints, looking unsure.

"*Goetia*," I utter. It's barely audible. But Grýla hears, turning.

For a moment, the walls disappear. The wooden cages, the large table, and the cornucopia of food disappear.

Grýla loses her grip on Miley, and the little girl bursts through the door and runs to the group of witches. Beth and Nancy grab her and step in front of her to protect her.

"*Goetia!*" I cry. I feel empowered again. "*Goetia!*"

I burst open my cage door.

"*Goetia! Goetia! Goetia!*"

The cabin disappears.

We're in a glade in the forest again. I look up and the moon and stars keep getting blocked by fluttering shadows. My devils. And surrounding the flying shadows are soaring black birds.

My friends finally see me. All of them, not just Maddie—the whole group of red- and black-robed witches are staring at us.

But it turns darker than night. And then I shudder as Grýla faces me. The old hag's eyes have turned a creepy pearly white again. And all the darkness, all my shadows, the dark magic, rush behind her. She grows twice her size. And standing beside her is that burly cat monster.

10

———————

WALPURGIS

I'm sitting at my booth in Hawthorne Sweets. This is the same booth I've sat in over the past week, but the restaurant is empty. It's dark with all those red and green Christmas lights switched off. Actually all the lights are out. That's odd. There's only a flickering yellow-and-red flame to my right.

Outside, through the window, naked women circle a large bonfire in the center of the narrow street. Some raise their arms to the sky, some hunch back and shake, but all are smiling and laughing. A few have their eyes wide open, staring, seemingly in madness. I recall my coven disrobing years ago and dancing like this under the power of mandrake or nightshade. But these nude witches are on a narrow street only a half mile from the university.

I realize I'm holding up a silver spoon matching the silver table, but there's no ice cream bowl. And there's hardly any silver on the table surface. The table is a mess, covered with mounds of spilled and melting dark chocolate ice cream.

A huge black bird leaps on the chocolatey goo, fluttering its wings and splashing some of it at my face. Then it dips its beak down over some of the melted ice cream. Before I can shoo the bird away, it flutters its wings again, spattering me some more. Then it darts off to my left.

The raven soars from the restaurant into a valley. That's so weird because, to my left, there should be a counter for fixing all the ice cream treats. But the wall on my left is gone.

In a valley of charred black dirt, thousands of naked people sit in rows, holding their knees as if in fetal position, the way we sat in Grýla's cages. Their skin is caked in dust and mud, like the Samhain Witch once was. Thousands sit in nearly perfect rows as if someone has gathered inmates or criminals and lined them up. They're the only thing present in the charred valley, except black hills on the far horizon. It's like a volcano with the only living things being the muddy people. It even smells of sulfur.

"They never stop their crying. Never ever."

I'd know that voice anywhere. It's Melanie! But across from me in the booth isn't the Melanie I saw in Savannah. Like the figures lined up in the valley, she's appearing as she once was—a muddy monster, naked, a thin-haired, filthy hag. A thin black snake slithers slowly along her neck. Her eyes are white amidst the mud, and her lips, curled in a smile, are cracked and gray. This is the Melanie I remember from when she was my archenemy—when she once tried to kill me. She looks terrifying.

"I told you, Cadence. They cry and cry and cry. That's what all people do." Although she looks hideous, it's the same normal voice, with a southern accent, I remember from Savannah. She glances at the valley. Then she shakes her head, looking down at the chocolaty mess on the table. "But I sure don't like ice cream."

"What's going on, Melanie? Are you conjuring this place?"

"Why would I do that? I don't like ice cream."

"What's happening? Why are we here?"

"Samhain sure don't like Christmas either," Melanie says, shaking her head. "All that red and green color is so fake. There's no hollies growing on top of chocolate or strawberry ice cream, I tell you."

"How can you help my friends?"

"Seems you're the one who needs help," Melanie says, staring out the window. "Seems things aren't going so well right now in Hawthorne. I thought they weren't. You know, witches cry and cry and cry, Cadence. You all need to just shut your goddamn mouths. That's what I told

Bonnie. I said to Bonnie, 'We'd all get along so much better in this world if half the whole world would just stop all their scrying.'"

Her madness is too much for me. I bury my head in my hands. How could she not be conjuring all this?

"Ever wonder why it's dark?" she asks, leaning forward. "Wonder why we travel through mazes come Christmas? Dark to left, fire to right; light candles, incense, upon bonfire light? *Lux Tenebris. Lux alba. Walpurgis. Walpurgis. Walpurgis.* Burn the witch. 'Burn 'em all.' Stop all the magic. And please, please, don't bring me back, Momma."

"What are you saying!" I snap. "Melanie, you have to help me! Just tell me what the hell's going on! Why am I here?"

She leaps over the table and grabs my arm. Her muddy fingers and long fingernails stab my wrist. I remember those sharp nails cutting my neck when she once tried to choke me to death.

"Stop it, Melanie! Stop it. They're trying to help you!"

Then she lets go of my arm and lands back in the booth. She crosses her arms. And then she just stares back at me.

I turn to my left and see that horrible dark valley again. It's like thousands of people suffering in hell. That makes me turn to my right—which is just as bad. There, naked witches keep lifting their arms, shaking their hips, and bouncing their breasts in drug-filled ecstasy. I have nowhere to turn.

"You sacrificed your life for me once, Cadence. So I came to sacrifice for you. Think Samhain wants to be casting again?" She wags a finger. "Stop your crying. I came here to cast magic for you. I sure don't like witches and I don't like ice cream, but Samhain came to help. Now tell her . . . why Walpurgis? Why do witches dance around flames come Walpurgis Night, Cadence Hawthorne?"

And then she just sits with folded arms and waits again. This filthy monster stares at me waiting for an answer, as if she's some wise man asking me to solve a riddle. If I weren't totally freaked out, perhaps it'd be funny.

When I don't answer, she even lifts her mud-caked brow.

"Walpurgis?" I ask. "Walpurgis night, Melanie? You're asking me about Walpurgis?"

"Walpurgis," she echoes with a nod. "Why do witches practice black sabbaths worshipping the devil beside fire, Cadence? Who do they worship under the light of the moon. Selene? Diana? Why do they dance around fire and moonlight? Why do all those sinful, terrible, wicked witches do that? Why did your teacher teach you to say *lux alba* when all that nasty witch ever did in her life was cast evil?"

But I put my head in my hands again, fighting back more tears. Maybe all this magic is a figment of my imagination? Including you. Maybe I'm just losing my mind, about to be killed by Grýla?

When I look up at Melanie, across from me, she's changed. She has pretty long blond hair, like when Maddie and I visited her at her house in Savannah. And she's wearing a lovely long draping saffron dress. She's giving me a gentle smile.

"Burn the witches," Melanie says gently with a nod. "*Walpurgis night,* Cadence. *Walpurgis. Walpurgis. Walpurgis.* You never saw this wicked witch dare show up in Samhain, did you? When there's imbalance, a witch casts a circle. Ouroboros. Snake. Your heart gets it. You cast one before entering her house. Now tell your mind. When Christmas comes all dark, when everything's dying in the snow from the cold, and all the crops wither and decay—people be dying too—what do all the folks celebrating Santa Claus do? Why all these stupid fake red and green lights? And all their children running to see Santa Claus with smiles? What are they smiling about? The cold snow? Their dead, decaying bodies? Their newest gold earrings or pressed pretty dress?" She shakes her head. "They turn darkness to light. They complete the circle of life."

She gestures to the dancers out our window.

"Why do you, Alondra, and Abigail light your candles by your chest? See them dancers? Why are witches always lighting fire in the darkest night, Hawthorne Witch? They dance around fire under moonlight. Moonlight, Windstorm. Selene. Diana. *Lux alba et tenebris,* my dear, sweet friend.

"But if you throw too much chocolate ice cream on the table, what do you get?" She gestures at the table. "A big fucking mess, if you ask me. Don't drag me back into this, Hassyhorn. I told you and Maddie back home that I don't like witches, and I sure don't like ice cream. I don't want to come down and cast magic ever again. Yule's been here ever since I learned witchcraft, but she could never tempt me or Alondra. Because

Samhain sure loved her magic and Alondra—" She chuckles. "Alondra loved herself. This witch can't trap you when you love something more than her temptations."

"I think I suggested this to Bryce," I mutter. "You're telling me Enora and I are empowering this witch with our dark magic? We're making her more powerful with dark necromancy. We're making her possession worse. We need to use light, not darkness to balance Hawthorne."

"Blessed be," she says, nodding and smiling. "You understand?"

"Yes, I think I do. Thank you."

I collect my thoughts, as my teacher once taught me. In deep concentration, I dip my head down and recite aloud:

"White light. Alba. Alba. Bring fire to reveal shadows. Darkness to light. Shadows to fire. Left to right. As below, so above. As above, so below. Reveal my shadows. Shine light upon her daemons and free her."

"Now you're getting it!" Melanie exclaims.

The red and green lights streamed along the restaurant walls switch on. Then come all the lights in the restaurant. The dead valley to my left vanishes. That waitress with the red Santa hat with a white pom-pom appears behind the ice cream counter, and it feels bright and warm. The chocolate ice cream smeared on my table disappears. And outside I see daylight with a normal view of the narrow road that heads to campus.

"Merry Christmas, Cadence," Melanie says, standing up in her long flowing golden dress. The dress matches her long blond hair. This once hideous, filthy witch now seems clean and beautiful with her flowing hair and soft skin. "Won't you come visit me with Madison in Savannah again? Friday is game night. They're not always serving bologna sandwiches, you know."

11

CLEAN UP MY MESS

I awaken to a growl. That makes me more disoriented than ever because it sounded like a lion in the forest. *Hawthorne Forest*. What the hell's a lion doing in my forest? A rush of yellow shoots through bushes and leaves, lunging at something in a grassy opening in the trees. It's a huge lion with a mane clawing at the old hag, Grýla! I'm not sure what looks more bizarre—a huge lion in snowy Hawthorne Forest or the old hag, twice her normal size, wrestling one. And it's not only the lion—ravens keep swooping down and pecking at the old witch too. A large group of black- and red-robed spectators are surrounding the fight, keeping their distance.

I'm leaning on my side in that pentacle of branches I designed. It's still dark. Even though the sun's rays keep trying to peek through the thick mist, it's dark as night. Hidden farther behind more trees, Kenosha and three witches in black robes, Nancy, Josie, and Beth, are standing in front of Miley, protecting her.

"Katie," says Maddie, crouching over me. "Katie, wake up."

"Cadence, are you all right?" asks Bryce. "We brought you inside the circle."

Seeing Bryce energizes me. He's not chained. He's even wearing his shirt and holding my book, *Broomstick*, under his arm.

"Where are the kids?" I ask with a nod. "Where's Cat?"

"There were more kids in the house?" Maddie asks. "Only this little girl ran out before it disappeared. We haven't seen Cat or any other kid. Only that horrible witch."

There's another growl.

"*Laugh in your grave!*" shouts a guttural voice.

That's Enora. She's talking as a lion, just like she did once while fighting me on campus. Enora *is* the lion. Grýla hurls her twenty yards into a tree trunk, splintering the tree. But the minute Grýla stands tall, a flock of ravens pounce on her. The lion growls, its sound echoing in the woods. Then she charges the witch, knocking her down and rolling with her again.

"We need to find the kids," I say, reaching for my friends to help me up. "We have to help them."

There's a yelp as the lion is thrown across the field into another tree. Then a large black cat the size of a panther leaps from the shadows and pounces on her. As more ravens crowd Grýla, the lion wrestles the large black cat.

I snatch my book from Bryce and walk out of my magic circle.

"Cadence, take it easy," warns Bryce. "Be careful!"

"*Manifesta,*" I say, raising my arms toward the lion. "*Manifesta! Manifesta Enora.*"

As the lion lunges for the black cat, Enora's transformed back into her human form in midair. Enora rolls away on the grass just in time to miss the black cat's teeth.

"*Igni!*" Mira shouts, holding her grimoire over the cat. "*Igni!*"

The black cat catches on fire. Then a swarm of red-robed witches quickly drag Enora out of the animal's reach.

Grýla isn't fighting her birds anymore. All of Enora's black birds are lying in the grass, shaking and twitching in a circle around the hag.

Enora pulls out her wand.

"Enora!" I shout. "Stop!" I reach out my hand and will her wand to fly out of her grasp. "Stop casting black magic! Our dark magic is empowering the witch!"

"Whose side are you on!" cries Cordelia. "Fighting against Master again?" Many other red-robed witches shout at me.

"You have to stop fighting with dark magic, guys!" I yell. I look up at the darkness above. "Away, daemons! Away! By Hecate, I call off this attack. And I call off Enora's magic upon my hallowed ground!"

My shadows disperse, freeing the sky. Bright rays from the sun make me squint, warming my face and brightening the whole forest. And then, Melanie's right. Grýla shrinks back to her normal height. And that beastly huge black cat turns back into a small Bombay cat, now smoking and rolling on the ground, dousing Mira's fire spell.

I'm viciously slugged in the face. *Oww!* I'm clutching my cheek and jaw as I fall to the ground. Shit, that hurt! *Oww!* Then, the infernal gargantuan tattooed-face bitch, Cordelia, jumps on top of me, crashing her fists against my face and chest. Bryce mercifully tears her off me.

"Stand down, Adder!" shouts Enora. "Okay, Katie, okay, if you've got some trick under your sleeve, do it now!"

"Where's Cat!" I shout at Grýla. "Where's Brittany? Where are all the children!"

Grýla straightens, staring at me with her creepy white eyes, brushes off the dirt, and leaves. "Is *Chandra* hungry?"

"Reveal your name, demon!" I shout. With both hands, I lift *Broomstick* before me again. "By the power upon this hallowed ground, *my* Hawthorne, I ask you to reveal your real name. This land might be your grounds, but this entire forest is mine. *Tell us your name. I command you!*"

"*Behemah,*" whispers the forest, "*Behemah, Behemah.*"

But Grýla says nothing, crouched down facing me, just creepily staring with her pearly-white eyes.

I wipe dampness from my face, where Cordelia hit me, expecting the salty taste of blood. But ... my lips taste weird. There's this strange mix of honey and marshmallow as I chew on something soft. It's ... it's a ... candy corn taste. Chandra is doing somersaults in my belly. Ever since I was a child, candy corn has been one of my favorite treats on Halloween. Apparently she likes it too. Images of bags of candy corn I ate as a child flood my mind. There was a special taste to the candy back then. You know, the taste of food changes over time. I'm not sure if it's our memory of the food, or if it's the manufacturer changing the recipe, but food never tastes as good as it once did. Well, the taste of this candy corn is amazing.

It tastes like the candy corn in the bag I stole from Damie when I was seven.

More sunlight glows on the base of a tree trunk, as if a floodlight is shining, illuminating a pile of candy corn.

I fall to the ground and crawl toward the tree trunk.

No, Chandra, no . . .

"Back in your cage," Grýla says, laughing. "Get back now, dear *Chandra*, so that you and Momma may have your fill of all my tasty treats."

A flash of light blinds me. Grýla screams. My eyes burn. And then my ears ring. That was my magical thunderbolt. *My windstorm.* I didn't hit her directly. I mean . . . I don't want to kill her; I want to exorcise her demon.

For a moment, sitting on the snowy grass, Grýla brings her face to her hands, shaking her head. Her wrath fades and she looks confused.

More thunder is heard under a cloudless sky.

"She's still tempting me with Chandra!" I cry, looking back at Enora and Kenosha. "I need help, guys. I don't think I can stop her without killing her! Willow, you and both Ravens can try. You three witches love magic more than anything else. You three can try to fight off her magic."

Grýla stands up. So I focus my intent and ready another lightning strike.

"Stay back!"

Grýla's creepy eyes glow a brighter white.

I have to save the kids. I just have to!

Don't you worry, I know what to do.

I quickly scuttle over on all fours to the tree trunk. I cup my hands and funnel as much of the candy corn into my mouth as I can. My baby dances in my belly again. I figure the more candy I eat, the more satisfied I'll be, and the easier it will be to fight her. Right? And that . . . honey-and-sugar taste is *so, so* sweet. Babies cry again. Or is that Cat?

Desperate, I recite the Lord's Prayer.

Then I shuffle more candy pieces in my mouth, licking and relishing the honey-sweet taste.

"*Exi seductor, Behemah!*" cry Mira, Kenosha and Enora in unison. Their voices echo in the woods. "*Behemah, leave this vessel. Behemah! Exi! Exi! Exi!*"

12

MARGARET

I HEAR THE SOUND OF CRYING. THIS TIME, IT'S NOT A BABY CRYING—IT'S A group of children. A dozen kids are standing in a circle in the trees, back where the cottage materialized, sobbing. The cottage is gone. All the witches, in black and red, are crouched down trying to comfort them. Raymond has Cat in his embrace.

I'm standing beside Bryce. He's holding me, but I feel so weak. The trees are spinning. I squint up at the sun; it's so bright above me in a clear sky. I love the warmth on my face—this bright light that Melanie suggested I conjure to stop the witch.

No, not my conjuring, it's always there. I simply removed my spell.

"Cadence?" asks Bryce.

I nod. But I can't stop shaking.

"We have to go home," Bryce says quietly, rubbing my arms and back. "You're shivering and the sun's falling."

"It's not just the cold. I'm still weak, Bryce."

"It's over, Cadence," says Cat, next to her dad. She jumps into my arms. "You did it. Thank you! You saved me. All the witches did. They fought her and her spell is over."

"Where is she, Cat?" I ask "Where's Grýla?"

"Not Grýla," Cat says with a smile, pointing. "Margaret."

Cat points to three witches—one in scarlet, two in black—huddled over an old lady in rags. It's Enora, Kenosha, and Mira. The old lady is sitting under them stroking the black fur of a Bombay cat in her arms.

"Margaret?" I ask, standing over the old lady.

Margaret just looks up, confused.

"She doesn't remember a thing, Cadence," Mira says, looking up from where she is huddling beside Margaret. "We're trying to help her, but she's so confused. She doesn't even know why we're in the forest."

Enora's surprised by a young lady with smeared black makeup barreling into her arms. Brittany, I presume?

"Well, Cadence," Enora says, holding Brittany. "Glad we didn't fight each other. I figured when you act your strangest, you're on to something."

"Thanks . . . I guess."

"Bye, my Amica. Send love and kisses to Willow."

"And where do you think you're going, Enora?" Kenosha asks, looking up from Margaret.

"I'm going to live happily ever after worshipping Satan in Atlanta," Enora says, putting an arm around Brittany and walking with her. "Bye bye." And all the red-robed witches of her Abaddon coven walk off with her. Brittany is still in Enora's arms, crying, as Enora says, with her back turned, "Till we meet again, Hawthorne witches."

"I really can't stand her," Maddie says. She's got that right. Then my face aches so bad. I'm suddenly reminded of her henchwoman Cordelia's vicious pummeling.

"Let's go home, Cadence," Bryce says.

But Kenosha is still crouched over Margaret. And Margaret is just petting her furry black cat, who is in her arms.

"Is there anything we can do for her, Kenosha?" Maddie asks.

"I'm hungry," Margaret says, looking up at me.

13

———

TOTALLY SANTA

"Wait a second, guys. Slow down. Don't open all your gifts at once. Ever since I was little, Damie and I have gone around the room passing out gifts and watching each person open their present one at a time."

"But that was just you and me, sis," my brother Damie says. "It's gonna take all night for the whole coven."

Damie's got a point there. There are like twenty of my friends packed in my living room—so many that a few people have to stand by the doorway. I even hear a few of my witches hanging out in the kitchen.

It's kind of fun to see my witches in festive Christmas clothes. Damien has on a corny red sweater and Maddie, beside him, is in a red V-necked T-shirt with a snowman. My hubby is standing beside me, close to our red and green Christmas tree, wearing a nice black short-sleeved button-down. He's enjoying some spiked egg nog he made (wish I could try it. No alcohol for you, sweetheart). Mira and Courtney are across from us on the sofa. I don't have to tell you what Mira's wearing, do I? The only time I ever saw Mira not wear black was at Dad's wedding. She's in a black dress. All the rest of the newbie witches are decking the halls too. Besties Beth and Nancy are with Gail and Noori, sitting on the floor around the sofa. Abella's cross-legged on the carpet. She chose the same witchy attire as Mira. All my friends in my circle are here for my Christmas Day get together.

"Okay, Cadence," Mira says, holding a large red box with a green ribbon. "Who first then?"

"Me."

We laugh.

"Just kidding," I say. "How about our dean?"

"That's okay, Cadence," Kenosha says dismissively, sitting by the sliding glass door. She's wigless in a lovely green dress.

I shake my head and move to stand up, but then I nearly fall. Cat and Raymond jump up to help me. Geesh, Chandra, are you getting so big that I can't rise? I reach down and grab a small, heavy violet felt box wrapped in a green bow under the tree and hand it to her with a smile.

"What's this?" asks Kenosha with a smile. She bounces it in her hand. "It feels heavy. You didn't have to get me a thing, Windstorm."

"Merry Christmas, Kenosha," I say, shaking my head. "It's from me and Bryce."

"Happy Yule," Kenosha says with a nod.

I turn to Bryce. He winks.

Kenosha pulls off the bow and opens the box, revealing a small crystal ball. It's not perfectly smooth, it has cracks in it. But all the red and green lights from my tree are so pretty reflected in it.

"I owed you a new one," I say.

She lifts it, bouncing the crystal and weighing it in her palm.

"I can't accept this," Kenosha says, staring at it. "This must be so expensive. This is real quartz, right? How could you and Bryce afford this?"

"We found it in a cabinet in Alondra's library upstairs," Bryce says. "I suppose, if you want, you could bring it back to Clotho to replace the one Katie broke in your coven in New Orleans?"

"Or just keep it for yourself," I say.

She doesn't look like she's returning anything. She can't stop staring into the sparkly glass. Kenosha reaches up for a hug, and Bryce and I dip down and embrace her.

Then shy Nancy opens a small box, revealing earrings. Bryce opens a box from me of his favorite cologne. And then all descends into chaos. Everybody's opening presents around me. *Oh, well.*

"Looks like we're just opening everything now," says Cat beside me with a grin. "Can I open mine?"

"Sure, go ahead, Cat," I say with a sigh.

There goes order. But, you know, everyone's smiling and looking so happy and I suppose that's all that really matters.

"Listen, guys," I say. But everybody's too busy opening presents. "Listen."

"Hey, everyone," Maddie shouts. "Everyone shut up! Cadence wants to say something."

"*Shut up!*" shouts Mira. "Go ahead, Cadence." Mira always knew how to clear a room.

But then everyone's staring at me. Some are midway through tearing off red and green wrapping paper.

"I . . ." Geesh, *everybody's* looking at me. "I just wanted to thank all of you for coming on Bryce's and my invitation. I love you all so much. No matter what happens in Hawthorne, it's always been about us. About our friendship and being together, you know. Just . . . Merry Christmas everyone."

"Merry Christmas!" shouts everyone.

Maddie smiles and nods. Then Damie finishes opening his gift beside her, completely oblivious. It's all right, we love him.

Bryce jumps up from the carpet and kisses my cheek.

"We all love you, Cadence," says Bryce.

"Hi, kids," says somebody walking into the living room. It's Aunt Jane and Dad. "Bryce. Cadence. We have a special surprise for you. Look who we brought along." And Aunt Jane gestures to a blond woman trailing her and Dad, looking like her twin, only about twenty years younger.

It's Melanie. She looks coy, nodding to everyone and smiling but not meeting anyone's gaze. Many in the room aren't smiling. Kenosha, for one, just lost all her joy.

"Hi," Melanie says, waving a hand. Both she and Aunt Jane are wearing lovely green dresses. I wonder if Melanie's dress was Aunt Jane's?

"Hi, Melanie," Maddie says. She walks over and hugs her. "I'm so glad you could come."

"Cadence invited me," she says, smiling at me.

"Hi, Melanie," I say. "Welcome." I walk over and hug her too. Then I hug Aunt Jane and Dad.

"Sure is cold outside," Melanie says to me. Aunt Jane helps her sit down on a plastic chair near the couch. "But it's nice and warm in Windstorm's house. Hi, Bryce. Good to be having ceremony with your witch circle indoors, where it's warm, this evening."

"This isn't a witch ceremony," Damie says.

"Welcome, Melanie," I repeat. Then I turn to Damie and quickly shake my head, shushing him.

"One gift at a time and everybody watches as we unwrap it," I repeat, heading back to my chair. "Okay?"

"Who next then, High Priestess?" asks Nancy.

"How 'bout you?"

"Let Mira go," Courtney says. "She's been holding it forever."

We all laugh. Mira rolls her eyes.

"Happy Yule, Meer," Courtney says with a laugh, hugging her tightly.

"Hey, isn't it true that witches celebrate Yule on the twenty-first of December?" Beth asks Kenosha. "Didn't we miss it?"

"Yuletide is twelve days, Beth," Kenosha says, shaking her head. "Many celebrate on the twenty-first, but many more celebrate at different times. In ancient times, pagans celebrated Yule for twelve nights. The Hawthorne coven under Alondra always celebrated throughout December, particularly on the last day. And, apparently, now under your new High Priestess—" She nods to me. "The Hawthorne coven celebrates Christmas Day too."

"We're all still getting together with the coven on the last night of Yule," Bryce says.

"It's an ice cream maker, Meer!" says Courtney. "Don't you just love it?"

"Thanks, Courtney," Mira says with a wry smile. "I guess."

No, she doesn't love it. It's really a gag gift, you know. You can't imagine how difficult it was to get those two here at my party to celebrate Christmas. Mira spends all year telling everyone how stupid and commercial Christmas is.

Melanie laughs at the gift. But then she just sits on the carpet with her back against the couch watching all our other friends open gifts. At times, I catch her glancing at me. But then I realize she's not really looking at me, she's looking behind me. Behind my lounge chair the sliding glass door reveals the dark evening in my backyard. She probably would have preferred that we meet outdoors. Because she's a witch. No matter what she says, Melanie will always be a witch. And witches love the outdoors, even when it's cold.

I get up and walk over to her. Then I kneel.

"Melanie," I ask quietly, almost in a whisper. "Were you with me in the forest a few days ago? Or was that just a vision in my head?"

"When?"

"When I was fighting Grýla? I had a vision of you in our ice cream parlor. You helped me by suggesting we stop all our dark magic. You helped us."

Melanie shrugs.

"Well, if it was you, I really want to thank you. You saved Cat and all of Hawthorne."

Melanie shrugs again. Then Melanie laughs as Courtney opens Mira's gift. It's a jar of water with a label on it reading "Hawthorne Christmas snow."

"Thank you, Melanie, for saving us," I say. And I hug her.

"I thought it was your friends who saved you?" Melanie asks with a nod. "Walpurgis, Cadence. Walpurgis. And Merry Christmas."

14

HAPPY YULE

Whiffs of lovely apple and cinnamon mist moisten my upper lip as I cup a small white mug in both hands by my face. As I walk, I'm drinking Abella's wonderful hot winter elixir. Umm, it's so yummy. It's a sweet apple cider. And the warmth on my face is so nice in the cold. But as we walk along the woodsy path, it's not just leaves and branches we're crunching with our flat black boots, you know, it's shards of ice. It snowed again last night.

Clouds pass by a half-moon overhead. A few snowflakes are still lightly falling among the trees, sprinkling more white fluff over our dirt forest path. I'm wearing two shirts, a sweater, and a witch robe with the hood over my head. So are all my other witches, because tonight in darkness, unlike so many other nights by our bonfire, our sabbath is done in walking meditation. But though walking, I'm still officiating with my coven.

"Blessed be," I say as we walk. "Blessed be the Hawthorne coven under Khione. *Lux alba et tenebris.* As we enter Yule, our longest night of darkness, look to your left and then look to your right." I turn to Bryce on my right and smile. Maddie, who's walking with Damie, cocks her head back and smiles under her hood in the white moonlight. "Although sight be dimmed, feel the warmth of each other through this blessed night. Our Yule season. Atman, witches."

"Atman," says Bryce, closing his eyes and nodding.

"Atman," echo the rest of my witches.

"And let Abbie's cider warm us through the fucking cold, Katesy," Maddie adds. "Brr, what a cold winter night."

We laugh.

"Sure, Maddie."

"Mira, just make sure you don't trip on the branches up there," Maddie hollers.

Mira and Courtney are leading this walking group. But they're not using flashlights, according to tradition.

"The moon is bright enough, Maddie," Mira says up ahead.

"Cadence needs to be careful with her baby," Bryce adds.

"I'm fine, Bryce," I say, rolling my eyes. But then my hubby reaches over to hold my free hand. And I love that.

"Witches," I say, returning to officiating, "darkness represents our longest evening. So when we walk, we don't only celebrate the blackness of night, we look forward to light. When in darkness in this season, we burn our Yule log. Fire from our logs represents the warmth that continues to burn into our new year. In ancient times, Yule logs were said to stay warm and bright for twelve days. Another tradition is the Yule Goat, where the city had to protect an effigy from arsonists. Why? Arsonists weren't just trying to destroy property. They wanted to burn the statue to bring the heat of the burning goat to the center of town to welcome the new year, guys. See, our warmth is like fire guarding us from the cold. Our togetherness. Let the love of this Hawthorne coven, our warmth together, cast away all our shadows."

"Atman, Windstorm," Mira says ahead of us, nodding.

"Atman," the High Wizard, my hubby, says with a nod.

"Katesy," Maddie says, "are you done doing your thing?"

"Sure, Maddie," I say with a laugh. "I guess."

"Well, you know Tammy is having her wedding in Jamaica? She and Nate are finally tying the knot. Ain't that fabs? That means that we all have to plan for the trip. She set a date between semesters so we could make it. Damie and I would love to invite as many of you as we can. I mean, we're all going, so I figure why not all of us go together and stay in the same hotel room, guys?"

"Maybe a couple hotel rooms," I object.

"Well, Katie can't go if she's too pregnant," Bryce says.

"I'll be fine, Bryce," I object, rolling my eyes. "Stop."

"We also have to still make it to New York City for Frida, guys," says quiet Helen, walking a couple witches behind me. "Don't forget she's getting married too."

"Don't get why y'all don't just go to city hall, sign papers, and be done with it," Mira says. "That's what Courtney and I did. Every time one of us gets married, it doesn't have to be all fancy-schmancy, like you and Katie's wedding."

"I thought their wedding was so beautiful, Meer," Courtney objects.

"Yeah, well."

We stop jibber-jabbering. And we walk in silence. But that's nice too. I let the steam rise from my cup along my cheeks and just walk. And it's soothing. With everyone silent, even all my quieter newbie witches, we all just crunch through leaves, branches, and ice along this broad dirt path, enjoying the sound of our boots.

"Just let Damie and me know," Maddie says. "It's easy-peasy planning for my responsible *doctor*."

Then she makes me nearly choke on my cider as she hugs and kisses my brother's lips in front of Bryce and me.

"Cat, this is what our coven is all about," I say, cocking my head back. She's following in the rear near Helen. "We just yap. Our weekly meetings are just about yapping."

"Sure, Cadence," Cat says. "No real magic ever happens in Hawthorne, right?"

We laugh.

"You guys are totally cool," Cat says. "And I totally want in the coven."

"After everything that happened?" asks Bryce.

"Yep. You bet I do."

"You can't, Cat," I reply. "I told you. There are too many witches in our coven already."

"Hey, I can see Josie's lights up ahead now!" interjects Beth. She's walking with Nancy, behind Cat. "We must be close!"

Bryce and I look. I have to squint without wearing glasses. I think Beth's right, I see a hazy yellow glow ahead.

"If you want into our coven so bad, ghost hunter, you can join," Mira says. "Helen, Josie, and Debra are graduating. We might need some of your friends next year."

"Shh!" I snap. "Come on, Mira. Don't get her excited." I put a finger over my lips, but I can't help but grow a smile due to Cat's enthusiasm. "Anyway, she needs to get into college first."

"I'm already in Hawthorne," Cat says. "I told you that, Cadence. But thanks, Raven, you know I'll do whatever I need to do to join. Do you guys do some weird initiation or something?"

In a large grassy glade, there are like a hundred small yellow candles lit in a large circle. We're on a cliff, similar to campus's famous Hilltop Bluff, but smaller, and four witches from our coven, Josie, Abella, Noori, and Gail stand near a low, simmering bonfire surrounded by unlit torches. They are waiting for us with big smiles. On one side of me is the thick forest, but on the other is this cliffside on a high elevation over the woods. Shadows of Hawthorne woods spread out for miles below. I can't make out my house, but it's somewhere down there. But I do spot the university lights in the far distance. And, if I squint hard enough, I can just make out the small black shadow of Hawthorne Lake. On the very far reaches of the horizon, there are shadows of mountains. The fire and all these candles under us seem so bright on the darkest night, particularly after my eyes have adjusted to the darkness. And that, not only the maze, but *that* is the point, you know.

"*Yatu*, Windstorm," says Josie with a big grin. "So how'd we do?"

"*Yatu*, Andrena," I say, putting my arms around Josie. "Are you kidding? It's absolutely amazing!"

"Well, I had a lot of help from the others," Josie says with a laugh.

"Took us all day, Cadence," says Abella.

"It looks so great, guys. This cider is amazing too, Abie."

"Who walks in first?" Bryce asks me. "We have to go in one at a time. And remember to walk with one candle by your chest."

"I'd like to go," Mira says. "But . . . Courtney can go before me."

"Thanks, Meer." Courtney kisses her cheek.

"Remember, really focus," I say. "Ground yourselves. We probably shouldn't have been yapping so much coming over, but now it's too late. Anyone who enters needs absolute silence. Walk slowly and carry your flame. Add the candle to the central Yule log. Then, they say, by the center, if blessed by Hecate, you will have gnosis. But you must remain quiet. That means—" I turn to my best friend, Maddie, and she scowls. "No yapping outside the maze either, Maddie."

Maddie sticks her tongue out at me.

"Do we have your permission to enter, High Priestess? High Wizard?" Mira asks excitedly.

Bryce and I nod.

Then we all watch Courtney slowly grab a candle, and she walks in first. Mira walks in slowly after her.

In contemplation, they both slowly make their way through the circular maze of candlelight. I let all our witches add their fire to the center of the maze. Then, finally, I take one last sip of cider, put it on the ground, and light my small candle.

The first thing I love is the warmth of my single candle by my chest. Then comes my surprise at how long the labyrinth seems. Even though the hillside is not that large, the winding of the maze makes the labyrinth of light much larger than it appears from the outside. I focus . . . I concentrate. I ground myself in meditation, concentrating on my inner light, meditating, as my teacher once taught me to do. Soon, I wander with little thought. I know you're still beside me, but all else is quiet. My friends have heeded my instructions. No one is saying a word.

I discover the center of the maze and place my candle down. Then I gaze up at the bright half-moon.

"Blessed be," I say pensively, nodding my head and looking up into the clouds and the moon above. "Glory be to God."

"Happy Yule, Windstorm!" they all shout, hugging one another.

"Merry Christmas, guys."

THE END

WITCHY ADVENTURES ARE CONTINUED IN OTHER BOOKS IN
THE HAWTHORNE UNIVERSITY WITCH SERIES

THE SERIES

- BROOMSTICK
- WINDSTORM
- THE HAWTHORNE WITCH
- WITCH MIRROR
- RAVENS
- SHADOW CAST

- ALONDRA 20 yr prequel

THE BOXED SET

- THE HAWTHORNE UNIVERSITY WITCH SERIES (1-3)
- THE HAWTHORNE UNIVERSITY WITCH SERIES (4-6)

***DON'T FORGET, EVERY BOOK IS NOW PERFORMED IN **AUDIOBOOK** FORMAT, NARRATED BY ALEXA ELMY (& PRESTON GEER IN ALONDRA)

PARTING WORDS

What did you think of *The Hawthorne University Witch Holiday Collection*? By placing a book review, you can inform others of your thoughts and help spread the word about my book.

Want more? Periodically I like to send news regarding current or new projects. If you'd like to be privy, I encourage you to sign up to my email newsletter. Your information will remain private and you can cancel any time.

Sign up at www.alhawke.com or scan the following QR code:

ALSO BY A.L. HAWKE

PARANORMAL ROMANCE

- THE HAWTHORNE UNIVERSITY WITCH SERIES (I-III)
- THE HAWTHORNE UNIVERSITY WITCH SERIES (4-6)
- SHADES
- HAUNTING JOY
- PHANTOM MASQUERADE

- MY EVIL EYE
- THE GUARDIAN
- NECTAR OF AMBROSIA
- CORA

FANTASY: THE AZURE SERIES

- HARMONIA
- CORA: RISE OF THE FALLEN GODDESS
- AZURE BLUE
- CORAL RED
- PRINCESS SOJOURN

SCIENCE FICTION

- CANDY SAVANT SERIES

Books available at https://alhawke.com/books

ABOUT THE AUTHOR

A.L. Hawke is the author of the bestselling Hawthorne University Witch series. The author lives in Southern California torching the midnight candle over lovers against a backdrop of machines, nymphs, magic, spice and mayhem. A.L. Hawke writes fantasy and romance spanning four thousand years, from pre-civilization to contemporary and beyond.

Visit A.L. Hawke at www.alhawke.com

Email: contact@alhawke.com

EXCERPT FROM BOOK I, WHERE IT ALL BEGINS...

"CHAPTER 1 - HER AFFLICTION" IN BROOMSTICK, BOOK 1 OF THE HAWTHORNE UNIVERSITY WITCH SERIES BY A.L. HAWKE

I feel a chill in the air. But the sunlight flickers between fall leaves warming me as I walk across campus with my best friend, Madison. It will be winter soon, but for now, the last days of autumn in Georgia seem so peaceful. I glimpse at patches of blue through the canopy of trees. The sky is like ... so perfect. I love fall, I really do.

But Maddie doesn't seem interested in Mother Nature. She's been acting like a witch since we got up, which is a bit odd because my BFF is one of the most energetic and cheery girls I know. I already asked her what's wrong, but she won't tell me.

We pass the dorms and climb the grassy hill at the center of campus. At the summit is the tallest building at Hawthorne University: our library. But we're not checking out books. A line of students snakes its way through a bunch of cute tables with burgundy umbrellas to the counter of our university coffee shop. I think the wait takes Maddie over the edge.

She finally starts spitting out the events of her evening. "I went out on a date with Patrick. You know, the guy in my film studies class." She told me about him before, emphasizing how tall and cute he is, but now she looks as if she bit into something sour. "I knew there was trouble the minute he picked me up in that filthy, dilapidated flatbed truck." (I'm not surprised. She's not a very good judge of character, you know). "We had this great tilapia chili dish and lime-green margaritas and everything was going fine until he reached under my skirt and touched my vagina." I look around me, biting my lip nervously. We're still standing in line, and she said the word *vagina* really loud. People are turning to look. Then Maddie tells me she hit him on the head. Patrick, acting like he was the victim, jumped up from their booth, ran, and left her the bill.

Anyway, Maddie's busy telling me this story about her date copping a feel—and saying the word *vagina* real loud—when, right before my eyes, she walks into the store and just grabs a drink off the counter. We haven't ordered anything yet. It looks like a latte, but I'm not sure. I'm not so sure she knows either. Then she grabs my arm and we make a hasty exit. Maddie is like a total kleptomaniac.

As we walk down a cement path paralleling the grassy hill, I stare at her and she flashes a really sweet grin, raising her cup as if in a toast. "Anyway, fuck him."

I'm thinking, *At least she was asked out on a date.*

She looks at the brew in her stolen cup, puzzled. Then she throws her long hair back and cocks her head toward me very earnestly, saying, "Alondra wants to meet you."

I'm still looking at her in shock.

"Why not?" Maddie asks. "It'll be fun."

But I'm not thinking about Alondra. I point at her cup.

"It's really good," she says with a chuckle. "I think it has soy. Want some? I don't usually order soy but…this isn't bad. Look, Katie…" (People call me Katie a lot, even though my name is Cadence.) "Alondra says she wants to meet you outside of class. Just come with me to her house."

"I don't know," I say. "I don't like the look of her."

Now we're dodging bodies on the crowded lawn, heading to the main hall of the university. The main drag of Hawthorne is a white paved sidewalk surrounded by grass and trees, with brick buildings on both sides— and even more college bodies. The classroom buildings are spread out through the fields and under the tall trees. The leaves are so pretty in red and orange. Fall is my favorite time of year because I love the colors.

Hawthorne University is in Georgia. It's a really nice college, and I'm lucky to have been accepted here. So is Maddie. Everyone has a book tucked under their arm or is carrying a backpack. I have a pink backpack decorated with a unicorn. Maddie has always thought it's a little too cute, but I think it's whimsical. It even has purple swirls around the straps. Maddie's carrying a small book, but I'm pretty sure she won't read it. She's not the best student.

"You should go," Maddie says again, sipping her stolen drink. She runs her free hand through her hair, which is long and black like mine. I reach for my hair and realize I put it in a bun this morning, so I just pat the top of my head like an idiot. Then I think about Maddie's being a poor judge of character and think to myself, *No. No way am I going to Alondra's.*

"Why do you do that?" I point to her cup.

Then she drinks some more with a large grin. Again, she offers me some, but I don't have a chance to taste it because a nerdy-looking boy with glasses sprints between us, nearly knocking down her mysterious drink.

"Hey!" Maddie yells. "Watch where the fuck you're going!" Then she turns back to me. "It's busy, Kate. We should have gone into town like I told you."

I shrug. "I thought we'd just spend the afternoon on the grass studying for midterms."

I must look hurt because Maddie giggles and runs her hand down my back. "Whatever. Whatever you want." Then she leans closer to me. "Just come with me tonight. Please. It'll be a lot of fun. Alondra's really nice. And I have a surprise."

"I don't know."

"Well..." Maddie walks off and stands under a really large tree. "You have to. For the surprise."

"Yeah? What?"

"Bryce will be there."

"So?"

"Whaddaya mean *so?*" she says. "You can't stop talking about him."

Of course Bryce will be there. He's my teaching assistant and is really hot. "You're just scared," I say. "Now you're trying to bribe me."

"I'm not scared, Cadence."

She plops down on the lawn, puts her book on her chest, and closes her eyes. I catch a glimpse of the book's cover. It features a burly man with rippling muscles and the title *Complete Me*. She's not studying.

"Just come," she says with her eyes closed. "I'll meet you back in our dorm at six to get ready."

"Are we eating there?"

"Yeah." Maddie laughs with her eyes still closed. "Alondra always has plenty to eat. Too much. She knows just how to fatten you up."

Dr. Alondra Johansen has a house in the middle of a thick forest, only a couple of miles from the university. It's rumored to have been built during the Civil War. I believe it. It's a white-columned two-story mansion with a large shaded patio and a beautiful paved walkway. It makes me think Scarlett O'Hara from *Gone with the Wind* is going to run down the steps, any minute, to greet us. Surrounding the walkway is a field of grass and tall trees, along with a garden full of white and red lilies. I like lilies. I don't like taking care of them, or any flowers for that matter, but I like looking at them. Especially in the wild. I like the outdoors. Always have.

A small wooden carriage, painted red, sits on a modern paved driveway alongside the property. Parked behind it is Dr. Johansen's dark gray Jaguar XJ. How does she own all this stuff? Some say she's the descendant of an old wealthy family. It can't be from her salary. She's my history professor.

There are others walking up the dirt walkway, mostly girls I recognize from class.

With all the grandeur of the mansion, I'm surprised to see Alondra herself greet us at the door. A long pitch-black cape is draped over a darker black silk shirt and slacks. She has long black hair like mine, hanging loosely in waves. This time I'm wearing my long hair down too. And like the times I've seen her in class, I'm struck by her eyes. Alondra has bright jade eyes, like jewels. Her skin is pale, much paler than mine, and for a moment I imagine that she's a vampire. It would certainly fit her affinity for the nineteenth century.

But her smile isn't sinister; it's sweet. She's always nice—too nice. She has a bright grin and seems thrilled to see me. "Cadence Hawthorne, come in." I'm a little surprised she remembers my name. "I'm so glad you came. Are you considering our project?"

"I'm thinking about it, Dr. Johansen."

Standing beside Alondra is her teaching assistant, the irresistibly yummy guy Maddie used to bribe me to come. Bryce's suit doesn't hide his muscular, athletic physique. He's looking down into my eyes too. But his eyes are blue—gorgeous blue. I'm reminded of the cover of that trashy romance novel my best friend was reading. The model was like a bulkier version of Bryce, but Bryce is the real deal—and incredibly hot.

Now I'm blushing.

"Cadence," Bryce says, taking my hand formally and tipping his head.

I'm cherry red.

Bryce turns to my friend. "Madison."

"Hi, Bryce," Maddie says. Then she looks at me and struggles not to laugh.

I look away.

The foyer is grand. Above me is this amazing chandelier. It's made of a hundred tiny crystals reflecting light. It's the most beautiful chandelier I've ever seen. I almost feel dizzy looking up at the twinkling crystals. But that doesn't do justice to the rest of the house. The hallway, including the wooden-railed stairway, is white, and marble columns frame the front door. Enormous windows extend from the ceilings to the travertine floor. The hallway leads to the kitchen, where everyone has gathered, their voices echoing through the house.

Dr. Johansen greets me as we linger just inside the doorway. "Please, call me Alondra." Oh yeah, my professor is still greeting me. Watching me. She's still looking at me with her mesmerizing green eyes. I completely forgot about her. I'm a little surprised she didn't say hello to Maddie. "You can reserve calling me by my title for when we're in class, Cadence," she says with a nod. "But here, please relax. Call me Alondra."

Oh shit, do I not look relaxed?

My eyes fall on Maddie. My BFF bitch has the largest grimace I've seen in weeks.

"Come in, you two," Alondra says. "Make yourselves at home."

Make yourselves at home. And Alondra really seems to mean it. Bryce leads me to the kitchen, leaving the other two behind.

The kitchen is just as lovely as the entryway, with steel stoves, and marble—like *real* marble—countertops. It's all tidy and neat. About fifteen people are gathered in a small adjoining dining room, talking and laughing, their voices echoing through the large open spaces.

"You can help me with the trays," Bryce says with this amused smile. I catch his eyes straying along my shoulders and down my elegant black dress. It looks like he's thinking of something other than the trays.

What's on your mind, Bryce? … Hope it's me.

"Sure," I say.

He collects glasses already full of champagne and places them on two trays. "How do you like our class?" he asks.

"It's good. I especially like ancient history and medieval times."

"Yeah," he says. "You know, I used to be interested in engineering, but that changed when I saw how much math I'd need to know." He chuckles. I ogle his lips and that to-die-for strong jawline as he laughs. I freeze for a second. I fight off a blush and hope he doesn't notice. "I suppose that's what fascinates me about witch trials," he says.

"It's all...fascinating," I say. "You really seem to be into Dr. Johansen's research."

He lifts the tray and places it in my hands. I'm extra careful, because my heart is beating so fast staring at those thick biceps, and the last thing I want to do is drop the tray. But Bryce is so cute.

TO BE CONTINUED IN BOOK I OF THE HAWTHORNE
UNIVERSITY WITCH SERIES